Praise for *Three*

"A heartwarming story of innocence, teenage angst, and self-discovery, *Three* vividly portrays the pivotal moments in Isabella Guerra's life as she struggles with boy crushes, breakups, and big dreams. Written with honesty and humor, it's an inspiring tale that illustrates the power of faith and family. A North Star for the young reader."

—Pamela Hamilton, award-winning author of
Lady Be Good

"Within *Three*'s beautiful prose lies a life story that is raw, real, and relatable. To the reader's benefit, Ms. Peña exposes experiences and emotions in a way that drives home the point that the reader is not alone, that learning to love ourselves as well as others is a universal pursuit. Even as a woman of a certain age, I immediately recognized myself in *Three*'s Isabella, yet without the self-reflective way in which she navigates the highs and lows of love and life. This is a moving, meaningful novel for young women."

—Beverly Ingle, author of *10 Little Rules for the*
Modern Southern Belle

"I LOVED it. Brenda Nicole Peña writes with such heart that I couldn't put *THREE* down. Thanks to Isabella Guerra's journey, Peña has created an honest and insightful road map for those awkward teenage years. Grounded by faith, Isabella used painful experiences to grow and become stronger, ultimately making her dreams come true. A must-read for mothers and daughters."

—Kathleen Reid, author of *Sunrise in Florence*

Three
by Brenda Nicole Peña

© Copyright 2021 Brenda Nicole Peña

ISBN 978-1-64663-373-9

This is a work of fiction. The characters are both actual and fictitious.
With the exception of verified historical events and persons, all inci-
dents, descriptions, dialogue and opinions expressed are the products
of the author's imagination and are not to be construed as real.

Published by

 köehlerbooks™

3705 Shore Drive
Virginia Beach, VA 23455
800-435-4811
www.koehlerbooks.com

three

Brenda Nicole Peña

VIRGINIA BEACH
CAPE CHARLES

To Lexie

Prologue

November Sundays are the best in the Dumbo district. Out here in New York, I always sense a bit of sparkle in the wind when I walk around Brooklyn Bridge Park and breathe in the fall weather. With both hands in my pockets and a quick tap to make sure my iPhone was still secured away, I couldn't help but take advantage of the outdoor splendor. My boyfriend, Adam, was meeting me later to organize a few boxes and trash bags of clothes in my new apartment. But before he came over, I needed some time to be alone. My family left a week ago after helping me move into my new place, so it's my time now to get accustomed to my new playground.

It was hard telling my parents goodbye, but even harder saying goodbye to my siblings. Although I've been in New York for three years now, nothing ever makes these moments of separation any easier. Whenever I see them, all I want is for my mom to braid my hair, my dad and brothers to play games with me, and for me and my sister to lock my bedroom door and start dancing. Sometimes I feel like I made the wrong decision and that I should move back to Kerrville and be comfortable with where I am. But a little voice always tells me to keep going.

When I was younger, I remember living in my grandparents' house with my aunts and uncles—eight of us squished into a tiny house I thought was a castle. My grandparents came to Texas from Mexico when my mother was born to chase the American dream, which meant bringing everyone you know and everything you own anywhere you can find. Although we were squished together, my family did what they needed to do to put food on the table. My *abuelita* and aunts raised me until I was about six years old while my parents were working numerous part-time jobs to make sure I was taken care of. For years I thought it was normal to live with your whole family. It wasn't until I was about eight years old that a kid at school told me I was poor. It didn't faze me. I think I was so loved by my family that I didn't feel in any way that I was missing out on life.

My favorite recurring memory with my family is our Sunday barbecues. Every weekend, my grandpa would cook fajitas, hot dogs, and corn on the cob. My *abuelita* stayed inside prepping the beans, rice, tortillas, and hot dog buns—all while making sure everyone was okay around the house. All my family would be on the patio with our two dogs, Oreo and Muñeca, and I would be dancing to Selena y Los Dinos with my aunt on the lawn. Those were the best days.

Now that I am on my own, moving into my new New York apartment definitely makes me pinch myself. I can't believe how different my life is. Times like these, when I'm taking my walks, really allow me to reflect on my life; where I have been, who I have become, and who helped me along my journey. I'd like to think I'm making my parents proud. I remember my mother telling me once that her dream for me was to graduate high school. I bet never in a million years would she have envisioned seeing me off living in a big city with so much more than a high school degree.

I am currently a public relations manager at a children's hospital downtown and contributing writer for *Big Apple Words,* an online periodical that spotlights New York City events, restaurants, and the city lifestyle. I have no pets, but a lot of plants and tend to think of myself as a fashionista because I always snag the best deals at Marshalls and vintage shops. *It's a gift, what can I say?*

Of course, my life did not just casually waltz its way into being like this. I, just like many, have gone through my share of trouble, discrimination, terrible jobs, and of course heartache. The great thing about life, though, is that it eventually gets better, even when deep in your heart it feels like it will not.

It's almost ten. I better start heading back.

As I walk along Clark Street, I see three teenage girls laughing as they walk together to the local coffee shop across the street. Step by step, iPhones glued to their hands, they seemed happy and in good spirits. One of the girls has a journal in her hand. *I love seeing that.*

Pulling out my key fob to get into my building, I smile at a stranger passing by. My Southern hospitality still hasn't caught on over here, so I'm used to receiving confused looks or being ignored when I smile. It keeps me with a goal though, to have someone new smile back. People probably think I'm creepy, though.

I walk a few steps down the brick hallway before getting into my apartment. A13.

As I open my apartment door, the open space gives me an immediate sense of tranquility. Seeing your home, even if it's temporary, is a different type of thrill because it's your personal space. I love seeing the open windows as soon as I walk in. To me, exposed red brick is a staple in New York-style apartments. Now, I'm finally renting a place with the ideal look I had always dreamed of.

I turn around to kick off my shoes only to find Adam standing outside my door with some beverages in one hand and a bag from my favorite bagel place a few blocks away. Looking at Adam, with his hazel-brown eyes and dark scruff, I smile and almost knock him over with my signature super-sized embrace.

"The coffee . . . oh, oh the tea . . ." he says mid-kiss, and I quickly jump back to help him unload the goodies he brought. Adam is so thoughtful, and his selflessness is natural. He never fails to open the door for me, offers me his coat on chilly days, and randomly surprises me with my favorite treats. You've got to appreciate a man's love.

After spending some time unwinding and enjoying each other's company, we begin organizing my boxes, my trash bags full of clothing, and the random items my mom brought me last week. Not to mention the homemade tortillas she left behind for us to snack on. *Thank goodness she left her recipe along with them to encourage me to learn.*

"Hmm, what's this back here?" I say to Adam as I look into one of the closets.

Adam quickly peeks in from the other room to say that it was an unmarked box he had put out of the way in the closet for me to go through when I had time. As he goes back to sort out the mess in my living room, I get curious. The ambiguity has sparked my interest. *How do I not remember what is in there?*

I happen to make the slick choice of overestimating my five-foot-four-inch capabilities by trying to reach the top of the closet shelves that hold the big, unmarked box I want to dissect. Of course I fall backward, dragging along with me the box and everything inside it. We both land in a heap. I should have waited for Adam to help me, but he is sorting some items in the other room. Besides, girl power, right?

"What was that?" Adam stumbles into my room. "Isabella, are you okay?"

"Oh, just me falling on my butt again." I smile.

Looking at my floor, I notice journals scattered everywhere. All of them were mine. A note has slipped out from the box and I pick it up in the midst of feeling disheveled. It is in my mom's handwriting.

> It's not how you start, but how you finish.
> Your dreams are coming true.
>
> Mom

My mother is so sneaky. I have been so busy rummaging through my stuff that I did not make time to sort through the items she left for me. But she knew I would find her note eventually.

It was something she would say to me all the time. *It's not how you start, but how you finish.* When I was growing up, I would always get down on myself for messing up on so many things: forgetting my lines for my theatre monologue, accidentally parallel parking my parents' car like a maniac, or getting a C on a science test I thought I studied enough for. A vivid memory of mine was my struggle figuring out how to apply for college. I was a good student but lacked resources. Although I tried many times to go to my guidance counselor for help with applying to colleges, there were so many students at my school that it felt impossible to get one-on-one time. Even more so, it was tough explaining to my parents how much things would cost and what the process would be. As the eldest grandchild in my family, I was determined to do everything necessary to be the first in my family to go to college. Although there were a lot of things I had to figure out on my own, my parents were always there to support me. Whether they had the answers or not, they gave me the support I needed to try. They weren't holding my hand step by step, but they were both present, and that in itself made all of the difference.

Reading my mother's note brings a quick smile to my face and I lie down on my back and giggle for a little bit, taking in my surroundings.

Adam comes toward me and kneels by my side. He holds my hand while his eyes comfort me.

"You need to be careful, Isabella." He kisses my forehead. "By the way, are these journals all yours?"

I quickly nod and turn red. I had told Adam that I kept journals in college and high school but had stopped after my master's program a few years ago. He picks up my mother's note and gently places it beside one of my bigger journals.

"This one has a lot of writing," he says. He starts to stack the rest all together and put them back in the empty box they fell from.

Little does he know, the journal he had noticed was the one I would stay up until midnight writing about my daily struggles of teenage drama and heartache. It contained memories of my first love and getting the C on that science test I mentioned earlier. The blue one with the paisley swirls all around it. *Yeah, that's the one.*

"Do you think you'll ever let me read one of your journals?" he gently asks.

My mind lingers for a bit. Exposing my deepest thoughts as a teenager and college student would be the ultimate trust fall in our relationship. I look back at him as he finishes stacking the rest of my journals in the box.

"One day," I say and give him a quick smile.

I call my mom later that night to thank her for my box of journals. My parents and siblings had just finished their drive back to Texas. They explored a few states along the way, but were happy to get back to their Tex-Mex food.

"We miss you already," Mom says.

"I miss y'all more."

✻✻✻

The next day, I decide to dive into my journals and see what I was so hung up about. I get my tea, place my mother's note on the fridge, and give Adam a kiss goodbye before rummaging through my boxes again. Today is my last day off before heading into the office on Tuesday.

Scanning through each page, I notice a common theme of my journals: they all highlighted love, loss, struggle, and hope. It was nothing to be embarrassed about, but it dawns on me that these pages could be an interesting stroll down memory lane. But as a writer, that's too surface level for my taste. *Maybe I can turn these pages into hope?*

Some people would just hide their stories, or simply let their boyfriend read them and be done with it, but not me—not this Isabella! I want to see if these stories can have some relatability. Who knows, maybe my vulnerability can inspire someone else?

My editor, Clara, started a new blog section of the *Big Apple Words'* website called *Bagels and Dreams*. Everyone has a story, which is why the goal of this new blog will feature personal stories from New York natives and visitors. She's been wanting me to contribute a few stories to share that could be relatable to readers. I've written a few, but I really had to dig deep to find inspiration. But now as I lay in my penguin pjs and banana socks,

I think I have something else I'd like to write for myself. Doing public relations for a hospital doesn't exactly scream creativity, and I want to try something new to spark my interest—something a little more personal. Besides, my editor is always telling me to dig deep with my writing. What could be deeper than writing about your past?

I read somewhere that we all fall in love three times. Your first love is the one who opens our heart, your second love is the very difficult one that you learn from, and your third love is the one that just feels right. Although this sounds pretty spot-on in my life, I think it goes a little deeper. There is more than just *love* that occurs throughout your life—your career, personal sacrifices, family matters, and so much more. However, if we are going to talk about love, we need to talk about two different types—the love for yourself and the love for others. I believe once you understand this, that is when your life begins to transform.

I know within these journals lies the story of my transformation from a girl to a woman. Most women have their truths written in their diaries, but many others have their secrets kept hidden within their hearts. Although I feel that not everyone may experience three loves in their life, I do believe everyone experiences at least three different transformations as they grow into the most authentic version of themselves. Although this path may not be exactly 100 percent for everyone, we all go through some type of journey that helps shape the type of person we are. Not to mention, the people you accept in your life are huge factors in your growth. Believe me, everyone has to go through a few sword fights and roadblocks until their story begins to piece together perfectly.

From my experience, nothing is an accident. Everything falls into place with intention and when you look back at your life, you cannot believe how in sync your world has become.

Don't get me wrong, there are absolutely areas in life that can make you feel like the world is crashing down on you, like you are lost and alone. I've been there. It's tough.

I know this may come off as a love life, overachiever memoir—but the truth is, my decisions weren't as cookie cutter as my parents would have hoped. You'll find out soon enough.

I have been blessed with so many wild obstacles in my life that one would hope that I learned from at least one of them. Thankfully I did, and I felt the need to share some of my personal stories with those who need it and are willing to listen.

These stories are tough, silly, and personal—just like me.

Here goes nothing.

Welcome to *Three*.

One

From the Beginning

Do you remember the person you were before you got your heart broken for the first time? As soon as I asked myself that question a mellow smile came to my face. A flood of memories took me back for a moment. Who knew such a magnificent question could hold such a delicate answer?

As I hold another journal in my hands, I begin to remember her; the girl I used to be. She was like a beautiful sunflower—delicate, pure to touch, and a little wild when her imagination would run free. Her insecurities were nonexistent, and she wanted to be friends with everyone she'd meet. She was a little shy at times, but such a happy and loving girl. Although she was very naïve and innocent, she never once felt that she was ever doing life wrong. It was a time when young Isabella thought a simple kiss on the lips was the furthest you could go with a boy and know that their kiss meant they were going to love you forever. She had no idea what cheating was and wasn't living in a world full of drama, perversion, and teenage angst. I remember her like a sweet melody, filling the air with a breeze so light and airy that every breath was a blissful joy. I remember her and I know I'll never feel her again.

When your heart hasn't yet been touched by love, it's a beautiful and delicate time. Of course, once you start passing the age of twelve or so, your mind starts to swirl a little bit more than usual. It's a time when you never want to be seen at the movie theater with your parents, but also beg them for money so you can buy Sour Patch Kids and Icees.

But when you are finally blindsided by Cupid's arrow, and are in the middle of puberty to go along with it, things are more real than what *High School Musical* ever taught you.

My first love, as many women may have experienced in their lifetime, was in high school. His name was Anthony and we were best friends. High school is such an awkward phase for everyone in their own way, but there are always moments that tend to take your breath away— whether good or bad. I would describe my moments as a solid fifty-fifty. Some days I'd feel on top of the world, other days not so much. All I knew at the time was that I was going to make every moment count.

I was fourteen years old when I started high school. I was one of the youngest in the class and personally loved being the baby of the group; it made me feel sort of cool in a way because I knew everyone was older and I was still able to be a part of the crowd.

I attended Washington High School. Our middle school was basically split in half when it came to which students would go to certain high schools, so I felt like I lost half of my friends when high school started, and I was not a happy camper. However, my three best friends at the time—Samantha, Ellie, and Sasha—were all going to Washington with me and it gave me some hope for the future.

There was a high school football game to start the school year about three weeks into the semester. I had never gone to a football game at the time but decided to go with Samantha to see what it was all about.

It was a Thursday night—definitely a big-kid move for me because I had never been out on a school night—and I carpooled with Samantha to the game. Her parents dropped us off and we went straight to the ticket stand to give them our two dollars. *We were off!* The Thursday night lights were beaming across the football field and bleachers. I had no idea who

Washington was playing and was too in awe at the fact that I was actually at a high school football game to really care. This was what high school was all about: friends, football, and going out on a school day.

Samantha was one of my best friends in middle school, so I was elated that she invited me to come out with her to experience our first game together. She also wanted to introduce me to her new friends from the freshman basketball team she had met at tryouts. She had made the team, of course, and couldn't wait to start practicing for their first game.

As the wind kept testing my balance on every step of the bleachers, I finally made my way to a seat right next to Samantha and her new friends. I was wearing a T-shirt and jeans with a basic gray sweater that was too small for my chubby frame. I was at that awkward stage of never having worn makeup in my life, but that night I asked permission to wear blush and mascara because I wanted to feel like a high schooler. My French braid intact and bobby pinned, I was ready for the game.

Meeting new people as a teenager is both exhilarating and horrifying. You try to act cool so that others want to be your friend, but still want to hide in the corner because you feel naturally shy. It's an odd feeling, plain and simple.

The reason I'm telling you this is because stepping out of my comfort zone and forcing myself to meet new people is exactly how this whole story began. After Samantha had introduced me to all her basketball friends, she pulled me into another conversation she was having with a boy named Caleb sitting a bleacher away from us. He was a freshman at Washington as well and was very sweet and funny. Come to think of it, I believe he was in one of Samantha's classes. The conversation led to a merging of friend groups on the football bleachers.

About five minutes passed and I ended up buying a hot dog from one of the vendors passing throughout the bleachers. As I handed the vendor my dad's five-dollar bill, I felt so cool. Washington scored a touchdown and the vibration of the bleachers escalated as fans cheered and stomped with joy. It was exhilarating.

"I'd like y'all to meet my friend, Anthony," Caleb said.

As I was taking the final bites of my ketchup-covered hotdog, I looked back to see a boy with a round, chubby face peek out from behind the corner of Caleb's hoodie. He had just walked up the bleachers to sit down next to Caleb. He had curly, dark hair, light blue eyes, and a Modest Mouse t-shirt.

I didn't think anything of him at first. I was just there to watch the game. I really didn't talk to boys much, just if they were in my class or if I needed something. I had a few guy friends in middle school, but it took time for me to get used to being comfortable around them. Even so, this wasn't anything too crazy for me to experience. I was, to be very honest, hit with the awkward stage hard in middle school and was never overwhelmed by the presence of boys. Never had a boyfriend, never been kissed, and had a bad case of baby fat all over my awkward body. The funny thing is that it never bothered me one bit. I truly got to experience middle school like a kid, and I loved it. Whenever I hear stories of people dating in middle school or falling in love, I get so bewildered at the idea because that just seems like such a grown-up move for a twelve-year-old. *Having a relationship at twelve?* I mean, seriously, enjoy your Capri Sun and do your homework.

I put my hot dog down, said a quick hello to Anthony, and then continued to finish my food. *I am not the type to let a snack go to waste!*

As the night progressed, Samantha was really in deep conversation with her newfound basketball friends, leaving me no choice but to watch the game and pretend like I was interested. At that point, Caleb and Anthony were sitting in the bleachers right in front of me and we began to talk.

We talked about school, we talked about the game—we even talked about the churches we went to. Anthony had just moved to Texas and had met Caleb at the school bus stop earlier this year. Turns out, they were next-door neighbors and have been inseparable since.

Then out of the blue, the basketball girls decided to shout at Caleb a question. Caleb could not hear them with all the noise, so he crawled up the bleachers to sit next to them for a while. Anthony and I were left in our little bleacher section with nothing left to do but watch the football game or talk to each other. Samantha was chatting up a storm to someone else, so that did not help either. We began to talk.

To be very honest, that was also the first time I had ever talked to a boy by myself. I'm usually in a group or had at least one other person join the conversation. But Anthony was listening to me, really listening to me, and I had never experienced that before. It's very random of me to say, but it was a nice change of pace for the night to have another companion to talk to. I have younger siblings but they don't really listen to me, so the idea of a random stranger giving me his full attention was different and I was starting to feel comfortable.

I remember feeling so grown up during that moment in time. There I was, on the bleachers with neither of my parents in sight. I was talking to a boy, surrounded by high schoolers, and just soaking it all in. It was a true high school experience.

The night was chilly, and the stadium lights were harsh, but Anthony and I kept on talking. It was all very innocent and engaging. We talked about his home state of Oklahoma and how their NBA team needed some work, along with the type of school clubs we wanted to join. I asked him about his family, and he asked me about mine; on top of that, he asked me what my favorite color was and what food I like to eat. We were so invested in each other's conversation that the game was nonexistent to us. Every time the crowd cheered, we cheered along with them and laughed together immediately after each cheer. We had no idea what was going on, but I loved it.

Samantha was still chatting away with the basketball girls, and I was enjoying the night. It got to a point, however, where I did tell Anthony that I felt bad for hogging up all his time and that we could join the other girls, so he didn't have to talk to me the whole time.

"I don't really care to talk to the other girls. I'm having fun talking to you," he said.

I felt a slight change in my stomach that I had never felt before. I was puzzled, but pleasantly, if that makes sense. I couldn't even look back into his eyes because I knew I was blushing. I didn't know how to handle that compliment.

"Do you have a cell phone? Maybe I can text you some time?" he said.

You could have knocked me over with a feather at that point. I was thrown off completely. For a split second, I felt like I had turned ghostly white and my face seemed to tighten up. Why would a boy want my number? I definitely felt like I was on another planet. But I decided to breathe out of my nose and turn my frozen face into a partial smile.

"Sure," I said. My heart was pounding.

That was my first time exchanging a number with a boy. And it was such a huge deal in my mind.

We swapped our Nokia and Motorola Razr flip phones and exchanged numbers. I warned Anthony about how I had a set monthly talk and text amount, so our communication had to be limited. My dad would have gone ballistic if he found out I was the reason for the ginormous bill on the T-Mobile Family plan, especially since having cell phones was just becoming the norm and text messages and minutes weren't unlimited. What a time to be alive.

Just then, Caleb came stomping back from the top of the bleachers—I had completely forgotten all about him and Samantha at that point—and joined us again to watch the final thirty seconds of the game. I cannot tell you if our high school won or lost, but one thing I can tell you is that my life changed forever after that night, and I never would have guessed it.

Anthony and I messaged each other later that night to acknowledge that it was nice meeting each other and hoped to meet up again at school. It was past ten o'clock that night, *way past my bedtime*, and I cut the conversation short to go to bed and save my text message limit. But once I said goodnight to Anthony, I couldn't go to sleep.

I didn't think I had a crush on Anthony but had definitely developed some type of feeling. I mean, he was nice and sweet. Did I mention he was the first boy to ask for my number? It was the curiosity of the whole situation that lured me in, and it felt incredibly unscripted. As a fourteen-year-old girl, I was overthinking so many things in my head that night. For that reason, I decided to shut my lights off again and try to get some sleep. Too bad our brains can't shut off that easily.

The next day at school, just like the universe works, I bumped into

Anthony during lunchtime. Ellie and I were walking to our lunch table with our plastic lunch trays in hand when I noticed Anthony and Caleb were coming right toward us. I had never bumped into them or even seen them at school those first few weeks, and now the universe was suddenly bringing them to me on a plate. Had they been there all along? Maybe I just wasn't looking.

"Hey!" Caleb said.

Anthony was right next to him in another band T-shirt—a band named Paramore that I was unfamiliar with at the time. I could feel his eyes on me, so I naturally tried to only make eye contact with Caleb instead because looking at Anthony made me feel uncomfortable.

"Hey guys," I said coyly. "I can't believe I've bumped into y'all! This is my friend Ellie."

Ellie waved hello with her fingers on the lunch tray and nudged me to go to our table to meet up with our other friends. She wasn't enthused. I still hadn't gotten up the courage to look Anthony in the eye at that point, but I could feel his eyes beaming at me.

"Well, maybe we can all eat lunch together soon!" said Caleb. *He's so nice.*

"Sounds great. You guys know where we are," I said as I let out an awkward laugh.

"See y'all later."

That's when I looked up at Anthony and gave him a smile. He looked like a deer in headlights when I courageously looked into his eyes. The fact that he didn't say a word spoke volumes in its own way.

After that random encounter, Ellie and I walked away to eat lunch with our friends. As I sat down at the table, I felt frazzled and confused. Ellie looked at me.

"Well, that was a little weird," she said.

"Yeah, it was," I said as I looked at my food tray.

My heart was pounding.

Halloween

Before I knew it, Halloween was right around the corner. The first two months of high school had truly been a time for change for me and my friends. Samantha started sitting with the basketball team at lunch, Ellie with the cheer team, and Sasha with her swim team friends. I was left to sit with the school newspaper team, and I wasn't complaining. I still would check in on the girls, but I knew from an early start that things were definitely going to start changing.

I made a new friend named Halie that was in the newspaper team with me. She was different from my middle school group of friends: she was a rebellious, wannabe punk. But she loved to write, just like me.

Halie and I had spent a lot of time together at the beginning of freshman year. She was the girl to introduce me to the early 2000s scene of punk rock, black eyeliner, and skater boys. My mom would later be upset about this, but in high school there's always someone to bring out your rebellious side.

Halloween fell on a weekend that year and my parents said I could hang out with Halie at her house. Halie lived in a very nice neighborhood, and I think that's the only reason my parents allowed me to go—not only to get awesome trick-or-treating done, but to hang out with children that had successful upbringings. I didn't grow up with a lot, so even knowing someone with a two-story house was mind-blowing to me.

There was just one problem: it was Halloween on a Saturday and Halie and I were bored. We were in the middle of watching a movie when I received a text from Anthony.

Happy Halloween!

What are u up 2?

I had not thought about Anthony in weeks—I hadn't even bumped into him since lunch that one time. I'd see Caleb around the hallways, but never Anthony. We had not texted each other since that one night. It was definitely a nice surprise hearing from him and told Halie immediately that Anthony had texted me.

"Oh, I know Anthony. He lives in my neighborhood. Ask him if he wants to meet up with us to go trick-or-treating?"

My eyes widened and heart dropped. I was not expecting a response like that from her. It was barely five o'clock and I was just expecting to watch movies and eat pizza. The thrill of seeing him checked another box from a new made-up list of mine I called "Things I Have Never Felt Before." It was a rush of an idea that excited me so much.

"Okay! That could be fun."

I texted Anthony after five minutes—I didn't want to seem desperate—and asked him if he would like to meet up since Halie said they lived in the same neighborhood. My mind wandered a bit at the idea of my parents finding out about me spending time with a boy, but I brushed it off quickly since I was going to be with Halie. I trusted her and myself that this was simply going to be a trick-or-treating night. He replied quickly.

Yeah! Come to my house and we can go trick-or-treating together.

Just like that, my typical Halloween night was taking an interesting turn.

To put my excitement into perspective, I was so giddy that I couldn't stand still from that moment on—like a soda bottle after shaking it up too much. We started playing the Boys Like Girls CD and jammed out in excitement. Halie asked me if something was going on between me and Anthony, and I immediately said no. But after that comment, I started to wonder.

When you're a teenage girl, your mind begins to make you overthink situations. Sadly, this issue would carry into my adult life. But freshman year of high school was the start of it all for me. I mean, I had been very flattered early on in the school year by Anthony when he had asked me for my number that one time, but that *Spring Awakening* feeling had fizzled out. At least until now.

This was my first time walking in a random neighborhood without an adult, and my parents weren't around to prevent me from seeing a boy. Everything about that moment was thrilling to me, especially since this was probably the most exciting thing to happen to me in my short life at that point.

Halie and I were getting ready for the night when I remembered I brought some of my mom's mascara in my small bag. Now that I was in high school, I knew I needed to start upping up my appearance, or at least I thought I needed to. Halie even let me use some of her blush and eyeliner.

I was excited to see Anthony again, but even more excited that I was doing something a *high schooler* would do. No parents were around. We did not even wear costumes—just brought Halie's empty pillowcases and masquerade masks her mom let us use. I just placed mine in my pillowcase when we started walking.

Halie knew where his house was so I was counting on her to lead the way. This was before GPS, Google Maps, and iPhones so my guess was as good as anyone else's on where to go.

As we walked closer and closer to his side of the neighborhood, the houses started to get bigger and more elegant. Decorated in artfully lit Halloween lights and fake cobwebs, every home was even more beautiful and enormous than the next. These homes were like nothing I had ever seen before in my life.

I grew up in a small house in South Texas with my grandparents, aunts and uncles, and two dogs. Like I said before, I was never aware we didn't have a lot because I was so loved. When my parents moved us out of the old neighborhood and to a more affluent area, it was like starting a new life all over again. They worked their butts off to raise me and my siblings in a better neighborhood. *Looks like it paid off because here I am trick-or-treating in the big houses!*

Now, back to the story.

There was a big, empty lot of green grass with a small-looking house on the other side of it.

"There's Anthony's house. We're almost there," Halie said.

I felt a little relief. His was the smallest house in the neighborhood and that made me feel less intimidated. But as we walked closer to the small house, I quickly realized it wasn't a small house at all. The small house I thought I was seeing was actually his *garage*! His real house was ginormous. Just beautiful. I was in complete awe and dumbfounded at the same time.

His home was lit up from the inside out. There were Halloween decorations—the good ones—stretched throughout the round driveway leading to their three-car garage. The white-brick home was two stories high with a blue balcony decorated with fake spider webbing and a huge plastic spider. It was amazing, spider webs and all.

Approaching my version of *MTV Cribs: Isabella's Reality Check Edition*, I saw the curly-haired boy I met a few months ago and my heart was happy. I felt excited to see Anthony and really allowed myself to come to terms with the fact that a boy may actually think I'm cool since he was the one to text me first. Everything else that had happened up until now was all fate, *right?*

I could tell he was excited to see me, too, because of the way he kept smiling at me and the deepness of his embrace when he hugged me. Freshman year of high school is about the time right before a boy has their growth spurt, so he wasn't that much taller than me—but it still made me feel comforted knowing he was as chubby and awkward as me.

Halie and Anthony had met on the bus, too, apparently. She was also friends with Caleb, and it was a nice full-circle moment for me knowing that my friends were all suddenly connected.

The night started out slow, as we tried to figure out what houses we wanted to approach. I was trying to start conversation where I could, which turned into an unsuccessful mess. As Anthony kept talking, I kept laughing uncontrollably at everything he would say because of how uncomfortable with excitement I was for being able to do something as wild as this. I react two ways when I am uncomfortable, I either turn into a hermit crab or laugh uncontrollably and look like an idiot. For some reason, I decided to go with the second one.

Anthony also said that Caleb was going to join us a little later after he was done trick-or-treating with his brother. Caleb had become Anthony's best friend since he moved Texas so anything they could possibly do together they would take advantage of. Besides, I was excited to have someone join our little Halloween adventure.

It was probably close to six thirty when Caleb joined us. We all decided to meet up at their neighborhood park and I was excited that the night was developing so well. Anthony and I were having a great time together. I was feeling a little bad for Halie because he and I were talking to each other the most. Luckily, Caleb joined so she had another talking buddy. Other kids from the neighborhood joined Caleb as well, so that was a nice change to the night.

"Hey, do you want to walk over here?" Anthony said and pointed to the tennis courts.

The sky was still a little bright and we were walking toward the neighborhood tennis courts. I was getting a little nervous because we were walking so close together. Although Halie, Caleb, and the neighborhood kids were still in sight, I had never technically been *this* alone with a boy. My heart began to pound again.

We started walking until we stopped at the back of the tennis courts. He looked at me with his sparkling blue eyes and I started to feel lightheaded. I looked at his eyes for a split second and then immediately looked down. My hands felt clammy, and my skin was getting hot. I was uncomfortably comfortable, if that makes sense.

He began to speak, but I could not comprehend a single word he was saying because I was too distracted with how close we were to each other. As he kept talking, I became overwhelmed with the idea that this could be my first kiss. The whole situation made me nervous.

He hugged me again, only this time I didn't look up at him. I felt so uneasy that even the skin under my nails was starting to sweat. He pulled back a little, but kept his arms around me.

"Have you ever been kissed?" he said.

I paused and took a deep breath.

"Nope. Never been kissed," I replied in record time.

"Really? Wow, I can't believe that. I think you're so pretty," he said.

Me? Pretty? Okay, Isabella . . . this boy is not playing around!

I thought that would be the moment he would lean in and kiss me, but all he did was stare into my puzzled brown eyes. I tried to unfreeze from my awkward stance. *I can't believe he thinks I'm pretty—no one has ever told me that, not even my parents.* My mind was going a million miles a minute thinking he could totally like me, which meant he accepted my chubby cheeks and awkwardness.

He started to inch his torso even closer to me in our loose embrace. I just stood there looking like a limp pickle.

He looked into my eyes again and then . . .

"Hey, guys! We're heading to the playground. Come on!" Halie yelled to us.

No first kiss.

Our moment was completely ruined, and I had Halie to thank for that, as well as my uncontrollable awkwardness. I jumped back away from Anthony's embrace. I felt the sticky sweat under my t-shirt and jeans. Anthony was clearly frustrated as we walked back to our friends on the playground. He didn't say a word to me.

The moon was out, and it was about time for my parents to start heading over to pick me up. My mom called me and told me she was on her way to the park I told her about. I told the group that I would be heading out in a few minutes.

I felt gutted in my stomach, a little confused, but definitely caught off guard at the quick turn of events that had happened in the span of what felt like seconds.

Anthony and I didn't speak that much after our tennis court kissing failure, and I was too embarrassed to bring anything up again. Halie kept looking over at me with her curious eyes and asked me if anything had happened between us. Anthony was talking to Caleb on the other side of the playground. Halie was talking so loudly to me that I didn't want her to make any more conversation about Anthony and me so I just told her no.

I had then made up my mind that I was going to walk back and try to talk to Anthony before I left, but before I could even make a move, I saw the lights of my mom's car driving up to greet us. As I slid into my mom's backseat and clicked my seatbelt, I waved to all of them and gave a final glance at Anthony. I smiled and he just stared at me. *Yup, he's still frustrated.*

Later that night, I received a text from Anthony saying that he had a fun night. We texted back and forth for the next thirty minutes before I fell fast asleep. What a day.

I want to tell you that everything worked out perfectly after that night, I really do. I want to tell you Anthony ended up being my first kiss. But to be very honest, he was not.

After that night, Anthony and I met up at school Monday morning where he asked me to be his girlfriend. I said yes and he was officially my very first boyfriend ever. We lasted a week and it's all my fault because I had suddenly turned boy crazy and developed a crush on someone else in my class. Plus, Anthony and I were just too shy around each other, to the point that we didn't have a lot to talk about. He never tried to kiss me, either. I felt we were better off as friends.

Anthony had officially been my first boyfriend, and my first ex-boyfriend, in a span of a week. To this day, I cannot believe that my very first relationship had a lifespan of a week. *A solid week.* At the time, I thought week-long relationships were normal. Silly girl.

My sudden stab-in-the-heart trick didn't stop us from being friendly, though. He ended up dating someone else a few months later, and that boy I ended up having a crush on in my class ended up being my first kiss, but all in all, Anthony and I were solid.

We texted a lot more often and spent time together with friends on the weekends; we developed a great friendship, and I truly enjoyed his company. He was like a best friend to me and I think he felt the same.

Puberty

Do you remember when your body started to change? It all starts in middle school, when your grown-up teeth finally fill the spacing of your baby gaps and your face is suddenly filled with pimples. Then *bam*! High school puberty hits you like a pile of bricks to your face. Of course, I had developed a massive running hobby during the summer and was feeling good about my body for once. One thing about going through puberty is that you tend to be more aware of your body—the hair, the odor, the sweat, and all the glorious pimples. But even more so, you begin to create a complex towards yourself, which can be dangerous for your mental health. But the summer before senior year, I was feeling good. I did a lot of exercise in my free time, reconnected with Ellie, started hanging out with a more positive group of friends, and didn't go on a date with a single boy over the summer. Anthony and I didn't text each other that much over break, but I was too distracted with so many other things that it didn't faze me. I was ready to continue to focus on my studies and myself. College was on my mind, and I wanted to make sure I didn't miss my opportunities. I did my second round of SATs over the summer with my extra study time and applications took over my brain, in a good way of course.

I know I mentioned that I was the first person in my family to graduate college. Well, this was the year that I was rooting for myself, and I didn't want any distractions. My parents didn't know the first thing about college or scholarships, so I would take the time I needed to research and dedicate any extra time I could find to writing college essays. It was a struggle finding my own way at that time, but I was determined.

I walked into my first day of school healthier and smarter. I was ready to take on the school year by storm and told myself that I wasn't going to ruin my studies and college applications with the distraction of boys.

On the first day of school, I realized I had lots of my friends in my classes and was very excited. Lunch period was great because Ellie and our friends were all together. Halie and I weren't as close to each other anymore, but definitely still friendly.

The first day ended pretty smoothly, without too much homework to get through, and I was excited to get a run in before dinner. Humidity was blazing everywhere as I was walking through the school courtyard heading to the parking lot to hop into my blue, 2002 Honda Civic. My last class had let out a little early, so I took the long walking route down the stairs. As I crossed under another awning over one of the school patios, there was a cool breeze that fanned the air. That's when I saw him.

Anthony was walking up the courtyard steps. He was talking to someone, but as we passed each other, he stopped his conversation and turned to me. Our eyes caught each other's, and he smiled.

He looked so different—taller, in shape, and dressed in better clothes. His smile was the same, though, only now gleaming and without braces. He still had his boyish, shaggy brown curls that almost covered his eyes. He said goodbye to his friend and started walking toward me. I let out a big sigh and waved over to him in excitement.

I gave him the biggest hug and didn't want to let go. We didn't even talk; we were just hugging for what felt like an hour. It was probably only thirty seconds, but my teenage brain was in a tizzy.

We broke our hug and looked directly at each other. Finally, we both had the confidence we needed in order to see each other's faces clearly once again. He was perfect to me, and I think he could see that in my eyes. My heart was pounding, and I forgot what to do with my hands.

"It's so great to see you! I can't believe we didn't meet up at all this summer," he said.

"Well, you totally could have texted me! But no worries, this summer was a really busy one for me," I said. He looked at me and shyly laughed, putting his hands in his pockets.

"By the way, you look really great. I see you definitely were working out this summer . . ." *Why, Isabella, why?* "I mean you've always been handsome, but I think you look great!" *Oh my gawd, Bella!*

Why did I say that? Beats me. It's just how I felt, and instead of keeping it to myself, I let my mouth vomit embarrassing words. But it was the truth. A lot of guys transformed before their senior year of high school, some even before that, he was the only one I really cared to notice.

(Side note: don't ever throw a side eye to a person in band class, science club, chess club, or any of those clubs and groups that don't seem to have a lot of super cute girls and guys. Believe me, puberty is a game changer, so make sure you're kind to everyone because you just never know who you'll end up crushing on later on in life.)

"Well, I think you've always been pretty, so there, you have me beat," Anthony said.

He looked at me as he said that and when I stared back, he blushed. It was adorable.

Although there were so many people around us, it felt like we were the only two people in the school. I was taken by his presence. Have you ever felt that feeling? You could be in a sea of people, but when the one person you want to be with is there, all you see is them. It's a blissful, rare feeling.

"We should catch up. Want to meet up tomorrow morning in the cafeteria so we can talk? I can text you," he said.

"Of course! I finally have unlimited texting," I said with a cheesy wink. *There I go again with the desperate zingers.*

In early September, Anthony asked me to be his girlfriend again—and he finally kissed me. This time, it was in the school courtyard when no one was around. It was everything I wanted at that moment and more.

For the next few weeks, our relationship was filled with car rides, dates to the movies, and my very first meal at Chipotle. We talked about college and the rival schools we were applying to. He let me drive his car because he wanted me to learn how to drive a stick shift. We spent time with friends on the weekends, and almost every Friday night we would grab dinner and then park his car in the nearest neighborhood park. We'd talk and make out until my nine-thirty curfew.

One night was a little different than the rest. He picked me up at my parent's house one Saturday evening. When the door opened, he had a surprise note for me on the passenger seat with my name on it. I was so excited to see what it was.

When I opened it up, it was a drawing of pink roses. Although it seemed like he was a talented artist, he confessed twenty seconds into the car ride that he sketched the drawing during class Friday because he thought I would like it.

"You said you wanted me to draw you something, so I drew pink roses because you love them," he said.

Now I know you must be rolling your eyes at this point—and for me to be blushing red like a Hot Tamale was ridiculous—but he had remembered that little request I had mentioned in passing. It was really sweet. I kissed him, and we were off, listening to the latest of Zedd for the rest of the night.

That night after dinner, we went to the park again, to make out of course, but to also lay on the outside of his car and look up at the sky. It was a beautiful night, and the weather was perfect. We were laughing and having the best time, as usual. It's true, seventeen is such a magical age in a way; you have so little responsibility in society but so much for yourself.

Our hands intertwined and we chatted about how different life was going to be in college. He had a dream of owning his own restaurant one day, and I was determined to become the most famous writer in the world.

When you're young, you have big dreams. It was nice talking about it with someone like him.

It was almost nine o'clock, so we rolled off the top of his car and said goodbye to the starry night. As he walked to open the car door for me, he looked back into my eyes with a focused stare.

"I love you," Anthony said.

His eyes were glued to mine. I naturally looked back at him and smiled so peacefully. Being with him was an incredibly unscripted type of feeling. When I heard those words come out of his mouth, my body tingled with excitement while my heart was beating fast. I had never felt this feeling before. I could tell he was nervous and wouldn't let go of my gaze. I felt so calm after him saying he loved me, and everything felt wonderful between us.

"I love you, too," I said and meant it.

I had never said that to a boy before. The feeling was so new and scary, but in the best kind of way. Being unexpected made the feeling even stronger. His actions reaffirmed the tingly feeling that I had never felt before around a boy. It was my first taste of love, and who better to experience it with than my best friend.

Anthony was my definition of love. He showed me a taste of what love felt like through his kindness and boyish charm. There is no other way to describe it but this: he opened my heart and ignited a fire I didn't know I had.

As months went by, everything was great between us. We celebrated Halloween as boyfriend and girlfriend, we went to homecoming together, and he gave me a heart necklace as a token of his love.

In a different light, it was interesting falling in love in high school when you don't have your complete freedom yet. Sure, when you have your own apartment and steady job you have the freedom to do what you want when you want, but when you're seventeen, things are a little different. Your relationship consists of seeing each other at school and hanging out at your parent's house and going on movie dates—unless you snuck out of the house, which I did, but that's beside the point.

My parents would make enchiladas or some kind of Tex-Mex dish every time Anthony came over. They wanted to engulf him into our culture, and it was pretty neat to see him embrace everything Mexican. I even had him come over to help him with his Spanish homework. Of course, my mom took over the lesson after the first thirty minutes of us sitting in the dining room. I didn't mind one bit because at that moment in time I felt so relieved that my family was opening up to my first serious boyfriend.

My dad's approval is everything, so my heart was pounding left and right at the idea of them meeting. When they did, it went a lot smoother than I had thought it would in my head. My dad was cracking jokes, talking to him about the PGA Tour, and college applications. He drilled Anthony about where he was taking me later, but other than that, I wasn't sweating too much.

It was a surreal moment for me when Anthony met my father. At that very moment, I felt in my heart that he could really be the person for me. I'd like to think every young teenager thinks that their first love is going to be their greatest love of all and that they will be together forever. At my core, this is what I hoped for.

First Times

"**D**o you think we're ever going to have sex?" I said one night after one of our park dates.

To be honest, I was very nervous about asking this question and the idea of it actually happening. We were alone, snuggled together in the bed of his new pick-up truck. I felt impulsive that night, and as an overthinker, I needed to know his answer. He was the only boy I ever thought this could be a possibility with, and I was curious to see what he thought.

"I don't know . . . maybe?" he said, nervously.

The whole thought of having sex actually came after receiving my college acceptance letter. I had been checking the mail every day after school to see if a letter from my dream school was waiting for me. After more than a month of crickets, I didn't bother to check anymore. It wasn't until my younger brother, Marcus, decided to check the mail. He was waiting for his gaming magazine, so he had his own teenage reasons to check the mail.

"Is, you got a letter from the University of Texas at Dallas," he said.

His demeanor hesitant, his eyes looked alert as he passed along my letter. My parents weren't home yet from work, and my sister was at my *abuelita's* house while my other brother was upstairs doing homework. I toyed with the idea of opening it then and there. If I was accepted, I would scream from the rooftops. If I wasn't, I could hide in my room until morning and not have to tell my parents. But, I knew I needed to open it. I slid open the dense envelope, clasping both hands along the envelope fold.

"Good luck," Marcus said, still standing anxiously in front of me.

I gave him a quick smile, took a deep breath, and opened the letter.

"Marcus, can you read it for me?" I had chickened out. "I don't think I can."

I placed my hands over my eyes as soon as I gave my fourteen-year-old brother my letter. For a split second, I felt lightheaded and overwhelmed with anxiety. I was thinking about my options of going to a community college or my backup schools to ease any anticipated feeling of defeat. I put all of my eggs in one basket in hopes of going to the University of Dallas, and I immediately regretted it at that moment. All of this negativity swarmed through me. The thought of my parents' disappointment filled my head. I had to tell my brother to hold on for just a bit because I felt like I needed a chair to sit on. I was being overly dramatic, but rightly so, in my opinion.

As I saw Marcus' face look down at the first page of the letter, my heart dropped.

"You did it, Is," Marcus yelled.

I turned to him and laughed hysterically. Tears filled my eyes as I got up from my chair. I lifted both of my hands up and let out a great sigh of relief. I looked at Marcus, who read the letter out loud, and opened my arms out for a big hug.

Right after that incredible moment, the front door to my house opened to both my parents, *abuelita*, and my baby sister. Everyone came home at the perfect time and my other brother, Issac, zoomed across the room to greet everyone.

Marcus waved my acceptance letter in the air. "*¡Mira!* Isabella did it!" My parents' eyes lit up. "Look at the letter—she got in!"

My mother was the first to hold out her hands to embrace me, while my *abuelita* followed. My dad took the letter from Marcus' hands and read the acceptance with my baby sister in his arms. Issac slid over to me with his Iron Man socks and gave me a high five. My dad decided to start up the barbecue pit to celebrate. My mother had leftover meat to make fajitas and, with my *abuelita's* help, we were hosting a whole feast in a matter of thirty minutes. My aunts and uncles called me and were on their way over to celebrate. It was a beautiful day and an unexplainable moment.

I called Anthony that night to tell him the news. The week before, he had been accepted into his dream school, so we were both ready to celebrate together. However, after we got off the phone, I couldn't help but think about what was going to happen next between us. In my mind, I thought we could really be together forever. Now that things were changing, could this still be true?

Sex. Such a personal and wildly confusing topic as a teenager. *Heck, even as an adult.* The thought of Anthony's touch never crossed my mind until I knew we would be apart after that summer.

I did not want to have sex. I didn't want to lose my virginity in high school and get pregnant. I was terrified of that. In the hallways of any high school, you hear and see so many perverted things that you begin to feel tainted by the expectation that you have to do sexual things. I was afraid— but more importantly—I was raised to not give myself away before marriage. Of course, this was easier to stand by when you didn't have a boyfriend.

My parents had me at a very young age no job, little education, and nowhere near ready for a baby. But they worked hard to keep me happy and away from temptation, which is why my parents were so protective. My dad would specifically monitor my curfew times, call my Nokia brick phone every hour, and forbid me from spending the night anywhere throughout the school year unless they knew the parents personally. I understood then that they didn't want me to make the same mistakes they did growing up. But boy oh boy, being a teenager in a relationship didn't make that easy.

My seventeen-year-old brain was not going to lie. I thought that if sex was a possibility, there would be no one else in the world that I would want to experience it with more than with Anthony.

I remember going to my youth group one Sunday evening. Pastor Ramirez was talking about purity rings and saving yourself for marriage. There were multiple kids already having sex in the class. I don't believe Pastor Ramirez was aware of this. I remember one student in my youth group bragging about how he lost his virginity at a church retreat. I was mortified.

Later that night, I prayed to God asking Him to please let me stay pure. If I were to slip up in any way, that He please let me stay with that one person my entire life so that I wouldn't be guilty of committing 100 percent of the sin. In my heart, I wanted to only be with one person for the rest of my life. This was my purity goal for myself. I prayed about this for more than an hour before I went to bed.

❊❊❊

It was a month before senior prom, and I was thinking of the perfect way to ask Anthony. Valentine's Day was that coming weekend, and I figured that could be the perfect time to do something fun.

The morning of Valentine's Day, I scrambled to put together the best *prom ask* my teenage heart could think of for my boyfriend. At our school, the boys asked the girls to the homecoming dances and the girls had to ask them to prom. I had never done this before, so I was just going with what people were telling me at that point.

Anthony and I were planning to spend Valentine's together by going to a restaurant, but I was meeting at his house first before celebrating. It was my first real Valentine's Day with someone special and I was happy it was with him.

I compiled all the money I had saved from doing extra laundry loads and begging my parents. Ideas circulated in and out of my brain before I came up with a great idea. A poem!

Roses are red,
Violets are blue.
Sugar is sweet,
And I can't get enough of you.

I ended the poem with *PROM?* written in big, black letters decorated in extra glitter to give it some pizazz. I wrote it on a huge red card made from a poster board I found at a local craft store in town and decorated it with hearts and swirls. My first real valentine, how exciting!

I drove to Anthony's mansion house later that day and felt giddy immediately. An hour before arriving, Anthony told me his parents weren't going to be home for a couple of hours, so we were going to have the house to ourselves. When he shared that information with me, I was terribly nervous. We had never been alone together in a house before; his parents or my parents were always home.

I wore a flowy pink blouse with some jeans to fit the Valentine's theme. I also wore my hair down for a change instead of my usual braid. I was excited to see him and ask him to prom officially—and even more excited to spend my first Valentine's Day with someone special. Still, being alone together lingered in the back of my mind as something scary, but I wasn't going to let my anxiety get the best of me.

Walking down his driveway, ginormous card in hand, I was nervous. I felt like I was sweating all over and that my face was flustered. I flattened my hair about five times in the span of thirty seconds, just to be safe. I even held a compact mirror in my purse to see myself in natural lighting before I had the guts to knock on the door.

Knock. Knock.

He opened the door in a cute polo shirt, and I jumped at him with my big card. He stumbled over. I was giddy and flushed with emotion.

"Happy Valentine's Day!" I yelled and smiled.

His eyes got wide and he smiled at me, then leaned in for a big kiss.

As I walked into the empty house, I decided to break my awkwardness by reading him aloud my poem, instead of him silently reading on his own. Of course, he said yes to going to prom with me and seemed impressed that I wrote him a poem.

"Do you want to go upstairs to my room? I can put your card there."

My eyes widened. Anthony was already making his way up the stairs before I could even answer. I just nodded and followed him up the stairs.

Every step I took, I felt my feet getting heavier and heavier. I was looking at the walls of photos to linger a little longer before I had to go into his room. My heart was pounding at that moment because we were alone in his house, and I had never been in a situation like this before in my life.

A bathroom. Pastel wooden trim. More pictures of him with his sisters. My eyes were set on everything else in that house except his room.

We made it up the stairs. He opened the white door to his room and led me in. I took a deep breath. Fixating my eyes on his made bed, I was drawn to a stuffed bear and chocolates waiting for me.

"Oh, I love it! Thank you so much!"

I grabbed the gifts and held onto the bear as I admired his posters and computer desk against the wall. About two minutes into roaming his room, I suddenly realized that I was subconsciously using the bear as a shield of some sort because I was afraid of Anthony getting any closer to me. My body wasn't ready.

"You have a really nice room," I said, trying to fill the silence.

I wandered along the walls and looked at his posters a second time, still clutching the bear for dear life.

Not only was this the first time for me to be alone with a boy in his house, but also alone with a boy in his room. *Ay*, my mom and dad would have killed me if they found out. Even worse, what would my *abuelita* think?

Anthony sat on his bed and patted his left hand on his red comforter, gesturing for me to come sit with him. At this point, we had been dating for a while and had known each other throughout high school. Things were getting pretty serious between us. I was trying to justify my actions in my head before walking toward him. He was my longest relationship ever and we were best friends. I was fine.

But I wasn't fine. I felt it in my heart that something could happen today, but I wasn't sure if I was ready to find out what. I gently placed the stuffed bear onto one of the chairs in his room and walked toward him and his bed. He looked at me, leaned in, and we slowly started to kiss. Deeper and deeper, we fell to our backs and kissed on his bed. Making out was fine, but then he started to touch more of me and my mind started to freak out.

As many of you can probably remember, your first time having any type of intimacy can make you feel a little caught off guard and uncomfortable; it definitely made me question myself about how much sin I was committing, but I equally wondered if I was doing any of this correctly. I felt like a lost puppy because the most we had ever done was make out some.

As much as I was into touching, I felt the most inexperienced in my whole entire life. He then took off his shirt and he laid on top of me, kissing my neck and holding my curves. Skin to skin—I had never felt that before.

As his hands began to wander, I remember a voice in my head saying *no*. That's when I stopped myself from touching him. I couldn't bear seeing or touching him any further. I felt wrong. I got up and immediately covered myself.

"I think we should stop," I said as I looked over to him.

I saw him looking directly up at the ceiling. He made a deep sigh while still lying on his bed before coming up and looking at me directly. I was fully covered by that point.

"It's okay, we don't have to do this," he said in a monotone voice.

We both got dressed in silence and then headed out to get pizza at a restaurant nearby. There was no consoling and no silly joking about the situation. I was hoping for a hug or something—anything but silence. I tried to break the ice and talk about anything I could think of, but I wasn't getting anything out of him. It was the longest ten-minute car ride of my life.

When we sat down at the pizza restaurant, I tried to talk to him about prom and what we could do to make that night special—coordinate colors and maybe rent a limo, that type of thing. He agreed with me and we stayed talking for the rest of the night. He was a little quiet, but I was trying to give him the benefit of the doubt since I basically gave him blue balls without knowing it.

We didn't talk at all about what had happened earlier, but I wasn't too concerned about it because it was something I had never experienced before. I thought the awkwardness was normal and the next day would feel just fine. I wanted to put it all in the past.

On the way back to his house, he blasted the latest Blue October album, leaving no room for extra conversation. When we got to his house, he pulled up next to my car near his driveway. I could see the side of his face staring into space as I was grabbing my things in his car. When I looked up, he didn't look at me and I knew something was wrong. But because this was my first real relationship, I didn't know how to handle it.

"I love you," I said as I was getting into my car.

No hug. No kiss.

"I love you, too," he said, and I drove off.

After that day, the normalcy never came back. We would still hang out on the weekends and meet up after class, but as much as I tried to get him to talk with me and act like himself, it just wasn't the same.

About three weeks after that infamous day, I remember noticing him texting other people while I was around him more often than usual. I didn't think too much of it, until I noticed it was another girl. One weekend passed where he went to a party and didn't invite me; he just told me about it and that he was going to go so I wouldn't be able to see him that Saturday. I was so hurt.

The week before prom we still hadn't coordinated anything at all. I knew in my heart something was not right. This was all a bad sign.

That Monday morning, Anthony texted me to tell me we needed to talk when we got to school. So I did what any teenage girl would do: I decided to dress really pretty that day to try to sway whatever *talk* he wanted to have.

I walked into the cafeteria to see him sitting with a group of his friends. I said hello and gave him a hug. He told me to follow him outside. Thinking of it now, it seems so stupid because everyone was probably watching us through the glass windows and being nosy. The weather was sunny and there was an open bench for us to sit on. Once we sat down, he looked directly at me with his icy blue eyes.

"This isn't working for me. I feel like we should break up with each other."

"I agree," I said immediately.

Honestly, I have no idea why I said that; I think I didn't want to feel like he had more power than I did, and I wanted to make him think that I didn't want to be with him either. The truth is, though, I wanted nothing more than to be with him and this was my terrible way of building some sort of defense mechanism.

"So, what are we going to do about prom? Are you still going?" I asked him.

"No, I'm not going. I figured that would be hard," he said.

"Yeah, I probably won't go either. If anything, maybe just with my friends or something." I casually slid that in there.

The silence was apparent, and I didn't cry at all, which was huge for me because I was such an emotional cry baby. I wish I would have taken the time to ask him why. Why did he want out? Why was he not happy with me? Why didn't he love me? But I didn't because I wanted to seem like I was okay.

We got up from the tables and he gave me a really big hug.

"We can still be best friends," he said. "You're my first love and I never want to lose you in my life. I can never forget you . . . like ever."

I looked up at him.

"I can't be your friend," I said.

He stared back at me in silence.

I gave him a big hug, kissed him on the cheek, and then walked away.

Anthony and I never really talked after that day. You know how in the movies where people who just broke up would somehow find their way back to each other? Well, that never happened during our breakup. We'd see each other down the hallways at school and immediately pretend we didn't. It was so juvenile, and I couldn't stand it. He had said that he loved me not too long before, and him pretending to not see me made everything feel like a lie.

He ended up going with another girl to the prom—the same girl he was texting while we were together the week before. I ended up going with one of my guy friends and a group of other friends, so when I saw him there it was very awkward. It was all a surprise to me and I was extremely hurt. I don't think I cried more in my life at the time than after that night seeing him dance with another girl.

Actually, yes I did. A month later he ended up dating another girl, a different one from prom, at the end of senior year. When I found out they had sex, my heart felt like it had been shot and shattered at the same time. I felt like I couldn't breathe and cried even more than I did after prom night. I kept that secret from everyone because at that point, people thought I had moved on.

Something changed in me when I heard about him losing his virginity to another girl. I started to get massively insecure and care way too much about my appearance. I began making myself throw up on purpose. I lost even more weight, was diagnosed with bulimia, and my anxiety started to overwhelm me in different ways. I felt so ugly and used. I toyed with the idea that if I had just slept with him, he would still be mine, and that thought killed me inside. I replayed the moments leading up to our breakup and lingered on our final words together. Over and over again, I would tear myself apart. Lastly, I kept thinking about if I had agreed to just be friends—but I stopped myself. How could someone just be friends with someone they loved?

Mexicana

When I was a little girl, my mother would always tell me to never slouch, study hard, not eat more than two barbacoa tacos at family meals, and be proud of who I am. However, when she wasn't looking, I would slouch a few times. I'd also work a deal with my *abuelita* that when I left the dinner table and act like I was done with my meal, she would have two more tacos waiting for me in the oven. I mean, have you had barbacoa tacos in Texas? They're the *best,* and so is my *abuelita*.

I'm saying this because even though I would bob and weave through my mother's teachings, I knew for sure that if I slacked in my studies and suddenly didn't appreciate my culture, my mother would come at me like a wasp attacking a squirrel. For this reason, I was always very prideful when it came to getting an A on my math test or celebrating the *Posada* during Christmas time because I knew that as long as I kept those items up, I'd be in the clear.

And don't get me started on Sunday mass. Although my parents didn't shove religion down our throats, they always reminded me and my siblings about the importance of faith. We were baptized in a Catholic church, received our holy communion, and I was confirmed when I was in high school. It was a big deal in my family and, being the eldest grandchild on my mother's side of the family, helped set an example for every sibling and cousin to follow.

I understand that not all Mexican families are Catholic, but it was a huge influence on our culture and household. We literally made the sign of the cross whenever we passed a church, walked out our door, were about to drive on the highway, or when we were about to take a test. I knew I needed to be right with the Lord as much as I could and was terrified if my mother ever thought I was straying.

Of course, life tests you. Sometimes the greatest experiences in life are the ones that you never wanted to begin with. In my case, it was an experience about how others perceived who I was.

I was devastated over the breakup of my first love. It was the first time I felt so low and helpless at the idea that I wasn't wanted by someone I cared about. So, I did what any heartbroken teenager would do: I fed into the attention of any boy who would pay attention to me—a dangerous situation.

I remember meeting a boy named Kyle at a friend's birthday party the summer before college. Kyle was tall and slender, had a cute smile, and had thick dark-blond hair that would swoosh like Zac Efron in *High School Musical*. This naturally made me swoon.

We would hang out at the park with some friends on the weekend together, go to the movies, and text during the week when I wasn't prepping for the fall semester. He kissed me after three weeks of hanging out and I felt myself getting on track to somewhat forgetting about Anthony.

One Friday night, Kyle asked me to come to a basketball game with him and his family. I thought this was really interesting for me to be meeting his family at such an early point in our new and casual relationship. Of course, I said yes and immediately became elated with happiness once again because teenage emotions are like light switches.

We were running late to the game and happened to get there just before halftime. I was nervous, but ultimately happy that I was spending time with Kyle in a new atmosphere. It was a nice change of pace, and I was looking forward to watching a game.

As I walked up the bleachers, I saw a group of four people stare at me with piercing eyes. Although there were tons of people around, you can always tell when someone is looking at you. I can't fully explain it, but it feels like a weight pressing on your body. They had no expression and looked at me up and down like I was an alien. I didn't let it faze me that much because I thought we were going to be walking straight past them. As luck would have it, we stopped at the same bleacher level as that glaring group and halftime had just been announced.

"Isabella, this is my family," Kyle said, pointing to the group that had just finished glaring at me during my bleacher walk.

My eyes widened and I managed a smile.

"Hello. Nice to meet y'all," I said shyly.

No one said hello. His father looked right at me and then left the seating area to get some popcorn. He never came back the rest of the evening. His mother didn't even make eye contact with me but gestured to her son for a hug and said aloud that she needed to talk to him.

The other two people present were his sister and brother. His brother conversed with me a bit, but his sister had her eyes on the game the whole time. I just found my place in the bleachers and didn't talk much but would see Kyle two rows ahead of me speaking with his mother. It must have been something serious because their conversation lasted through halftime. When he finally stepped away from his mother's bench, he sat next to me and just smiled. His sister then moved up two rows to be next to their mother. His brother stayed behind with us.

After almost two hours, the game ended, and I was relieved at the idea of going home. Kyle and I didn't talk as much, but I felt that since we were with his family it would be best for him to take the lead in conversation and include me at the right moments. Even when I tried to talk to his family, I would just get the cold shoulder. His mother never turned around to interact with me, and I wanted to go home.

On the car drive back, it was quieter than usual. He said he needed to be back home soon after he dropped me off, so he decided to speed on a few roads. This ultimately ended up with him being pulled over for speeding and me panicking. I had never been pulled over before, so it was all a new experience. The officer let him off with a warning, and we drove off. Kyle kept telling me I should have started crying or something to speed up the process with the officer. He seemed determined to drop me off as soon as possible. I slightly laughed and stayed quiet the rest of the drive.

As we pulled up to the front of my parent's house, Kyle asked me a question.

"Are you Mexican?" he said very bluntly.

"Um, yes. I thought you knew?" I said confused.

The expression on his face made me feel like I had just pulled a dead rabbit out of a hat. He looked at me with wide eyes and then put his hands back on the wheel.

"I need to get back home. Enjoy your night," he said coldly.

We didn't kiss or hug. I got out of the car and didn't think twice about the words that were exchanged between us. I didn't feel like I said anything wrong and understood that he needed to be back home, but I did find it odd that he asked me about my ethnicity so abruptly. I was confused and began to replay every instant of that night. Although it didn't go as well as I had hoped, I was at least hopeful that everything between me and Kyle was still okay.

The next day I got a text message from Kyle.

Bella, I can't date you. My parents and I agreed that I shouldn't see you anymore. I didn't realize you were Mexican. I just can't do this. It's too gross. Sorry. Don't contact me again.

I'm not kidding.

When I read the message that day, I was in shock. I couldn't even cry because I was in such disbelief. Can you imagine hearing that from someone? Especially at seventeen. It was another eye-opening experience for me that I will never forget. His words made me feel even more worthless than my breakup with Anthony, which resulted in even lower self-esteem.

At the time, I didn't know how to handle that comment. I didn't tell my family and was embarrassed to tell any of my friends. What made it worse was that I couldn't believe I went out with him after reading his words. But was he right? Maybe Anthony broke up with me because I was Mexican too.

For weeks I found myself trying to change my appearance, cut my hair, or convince my mother for highlights. I wanted my race to be ambiguous and I tried to stay out of the sun as much as possible. I started making myself throw up again on purpose because I felt that was the only way I would become more attractive. My mind was consumed by the idea that I was someone disgusting and blamed who I was for the reason Anthony and I weren't together.

When I should have been focusing on getting ready for my freshman year of college, I wasn't—a huge mistake for any teenager to make. I had already gotten into the university I wanted, but I knew my social life and relationship status on Facebook were more important at the time. I was lost and would zone out daily, daydreaming of what I could do to make myself beautiful. I was looking at life all wrong and I didn't even care.

I close my laptop for the night and watch the city lights from outside my apartment window. I reply to a few text messages from my friends and Adam and lie down on my blue couch with my Texas-print pillow. With my arms heavily swaying to the floor of my apartment, a wave of sadness overcomes me.

Here I am, twenty-nine and on my own, reliving my story again. I can't describe it but reading the words from my seventeen-year-old self and the emotions of being discriminated against again feels ominous. Although this is now in the past, it aches to relive this story again.

God's Time

So many emotions were spiraling out of control at that moment in my life after the breakup and terrible text message. And just like every other Mexican mother in the world, mine could sense my depression and sadness in an instant. She had a sixth sense that could always detect when her children were off their game—especially when it came to me.

One weekend during summer, my mother ended up forcing me to go on a youth retreat at our church. I initially resisted the idea of going and ruining my summer by mingling with a bunch of strangers like any other seventeen-year-old would naturally, but my mom couldn't care less and dropped me off at the front doors of the church. I was so annoyed and anxious because I needed to get ready for fall semester! And to be very honest, I was also terrified.

Why was I terrified? Well, I was going in with two blurry eyes. I had been doing so much wrong that I felt like being inside of the church was disrespectful of me. I was low and my self-esteem was shot by the words from Kyle's text message. It was hard for me to look in the mirror after those comments. They would just repeat over and over again in my head.

I knew I needed change, but I didn't want to own up to it.

Have you ever felt lost in your faith? That very moment I was, and I never truly realized it. I believed in God and went to church whenever I could, but I didn't think twice that I was any different from the people around me. Some of my friends were believers and others I never really asked. But ultimately, my morals were straightened out to love God, love your neighbor, love yourself, and don't have sex before marriage. Since I technically hadn't had full-blown sex at seventeen, I felt at ease with my morals, but still very guilty nevertheless.

Walking through those church doors my guilt circled around me like a vulture, until I encountered some friendly faces at the sign-in booth. They welcomed me into this gorgeous study space where I saw other teenagers like myself, mingling in groups and pairs. No one was left out.

Now I don't want to say too much about my retreat, only because it was very sacred, and the items presented at retreats are spiritually private. I will say that our phones were taken away and were returned at the end of the weekend. All the girls were roomed with other girls our age from different schools and the leadership at the retreat created a safe space for everyone to connect and grow.

I always believed in God, but after my experience I could feel Him. He opened my eyes that weekend and made me realize that everything I was going through was nothing I couldn't handle. He never gives us obstacles we cannot handle. I realized that who I am and the Mexican culture I have been graced with in my life is a true blessing—and no one could take that away from me.

Coming home after that retreat, I felt like a new person. I gave my mom the biggest hug and thanked her immensely for making me go on the church retreat. I was full of joy. Sadness had left me, and I was at peace with myself and my surroundings. I knew everything was going to be okay and the idea of Anthony didn't cross my mind the rest of summer.

Although the retreat changed my life forever, I will never forget the gutted feeling I felt when I came back to reality at the end of summer. I was high on Jesus and was at peace with myself, but when I walked through the doors of my dorm room and campus hallways at the end of summer, all I felt was sin. Sin was what kept toying with my happiness, and I felt the significance of that as I started college.

From then on, I found myself more conscious of my decisions and my actions toward others. I began to see my value more and more, but the insecurity was still there, only blanketed. I had hope, but when I would see Anthony on social media, my mind would spiral into a weak confusion. I did see him before leaving for college at a friend's pool party before we all went our separate ways. I didn't lose my breath or suddenly begin to cry at the sight of him. Knowing he was there made me feel at peace with our decision, but when I would look at his blue eyes from a distance, my heart would hurt.

First loves are hard. They are hard because you can't compare the experience to anything else in your life. It is your very first shot at being vulnerable and hoping for the best. But everyone goes through it in their own, special way. Thankfully, you grow from the experience.

Time, prayer, and distraction did wonders for me—especially going away to college. When I received my acceptance letter, I knew it was God giving me another chance at a new and exciting beginning. Not just for me, but for my family as well. I was turning into the trailblazer I was hoping to become and hoped that my small success would reciprocate as a big thank you to my parents for pushing me to prioritize education and its value.

Being away from my hometown, I started to sense a new direction for myself and free my heart from a boy that I had to accept would never love me again. I missed my family all the time, but I could sense my growth starting to appear. Although college began to expose me to new ways of sin, I reminded myself of my morals and that one boy did not determine my worth.

Don't get me wrong, I still loved him. I loved Anthony very much, but he did not and will not ever have the power to take over that much of my soul again. Besides, I couldn't linger on the thought of *what if* anymore. He didn't love me. Maybe he had at one time, but he didn't anymore.

It was time to let go.

✳✳✳

It's a blessing and a curse to be able to experience so many intoxicating emotions at once, especially while trying to find your way as a young adult. Looking through those journals and reliving those experiences on paper was more difficult than I thought it would be as well, but I realized how necessary it was to talk about the sexual stuff and curious mentality—as well as the power of saying *no*. As a teenager, all you want to feel is accepted. Even though I said no to the boy I loved and stayed true to my morals, I still ended up feeling terrible inside. The sin surrounding that feeling ate me up and made me vulnerable. I became desperate to take my actions back at that point in time.

But now that I've reflected on my journal entries, it was the best thing I could have done. I said no and moved forward. I said no not just to sex, but to a boy I loved—which was hard. I'm not going to lie, it was all very difficult, and before being forced to go on a church retreat by my mother, I was using every guy I met as a new excuse to get over Anthony.

Meeting Kyle was also a very valuable lesson to me in the short time that I knew him. I asked myself all the time if he was right. Was I disgusting? The answer to that is a big, fat NO. Being Mexican is not disgusting. And as far as I am concerned, embracing who you are is beautiful and important.

Kyle's story, although sad, was a huge turning point in my life. I was exposed to discrimination in a way that I had never experienced before. Even worse, I let him have control over my mind for that moment because I believed that I wasn't good enough to be around him or his family.

As much as I wish that no boy or girl ever had to experience prejudice and racism in their lives, I know that is simply not realistic. And for this reason, I wanted to share another valuable lesson that I always knew about but needed to practice even more.

The lesson is to be kind. Be kind to those that are different than you. Be kind to people who bring you ill will, even if you don't want to. And more importantly, be kind to yourself. As you can probably guess by now, I didn't let this boy and his family bring me down for too long. But imagine if I had. Imagine if I had believed that I was disgusting for even longer than that moment? Even more so, imagine if I had stereotyped every man outside of my culture and decided that they were racist just because I had a bad experience with one boy when I was seventeen. I won't do that.

Take your lessons, learn from them, and keep growing. This story was too important to leave out, so I had to make a sidetrack. But the experience ultimately made me stronger in the best way I could have imagined and made me even more proud of who I am.

Reflecting on this, I wish I could just let my younger self know that everything is going to be alright. Don't you feel that way sometimes? That you wish you could give your younger self hints for the future.

I decided to look at old photos of myself. One by one, I keep seeing a girl holding a smile when the faces surrounding her had no idea the turmoil going on in her head. But there was a light; it was God that shined a light within me to keep going. My mom was used as a messenger from the Lord Himself to whisper in her ear that her daughter was in trouble. It was the will within that I felt gave me the courage to just be myself.

Does being yourself take courage? I believe so. And the thing about it is that once you face yourself and acknowledge your courage, you're unstoppable. In full transparency, the vulnerability you feel when you're young is something you have to experience to believe. In this case, the feelings were real, and the choices made all became important lessons. I'm not perfect. Neither are you, but our imperfections are what mold you into the greatest version of yourself.

Two

The Mystery Boy

When you stop looking for something, eventually it finds you. At least that's how I would describe the next chapter of my love life. But as I begin to open my journal and read a new chapter of my past, I find myself filled with anxiety.

When I get anxious, I go for a run. And since it's a bit chilly outside, I feel like I need to at least stretch or something before I dive into this next story. My heart is racing. I feel like Eminem's character, Rabbit, in the movie *8 Mile* when he is getting ready for his final rap battle. Both of my palms are sweaty, knees are weak, and my arms definitely feel heavy—no spaghetti though.

Although it is chilly, it's such a beautiful day. The big window above my desk overlooks the concrete jungle of Dumbo, and holiday decorations are starting to scatter across the way. There is a big oak tree sprouting tinted orange leaves—a picturesque view to calm my anxiety. My phone vibrates with a text message from Adam checking in.

I remember when I used to beg for a guy to say hello to me. Or even remember to call. Now, I don't have to. According to Google, it takes at least twenty-five years for men and women to have fully developed brains, give or take. Going into my thirtieth year, I now understand the growing pains of immaturity and the value of experience in order to make good decisions. But we all have to learn the hard way at some point.

Writing this allows me to release myself from my past. I want to go into thirty knowing that I'm okay with everything that has happened to me, in some shape or form. But this next story is not something I want to relive again. But I will.

When I was nineteen years old and a sophomore in college, I was embracing college life and enjoyed not being around my parents all the time. I was making new friends, creating new memories, and exploring a new city. Single, young, and a girl on the rise. That's what I would try to tell myself at least. School was going well, and I had managed to take a very much-needed break from boys. It was my last year as a teenager and I was on the cusp of feeling like a full-on adult. I was focused on graduating on time, instead of becoming a super senior and graduating in ten years instead of four. I decided to scrape up some extra grant and scholarship money to take summer courses and stay on track with my degree plan. To accomplish this, I went back home for the summer to take some classes at a local community college during break and save money.

In one of my summer classes, I befriended a girl named Jessica. She was very kind and we got along well. One day after class, we decided to walk together to our cars when she asked me if I had a boyfriend. I told her no but was caught off guard with the question.

"I want you to meet someone. He's taking summer classes just like you and is looking for more people to meet."

The idea of this excited me, and I had a few more weeks until I had to go back to campus in Dallas. One part of me didn't want to meet him and just wanted to focus on getting my summer classes out of the way. On the other hand, I was curious.

"Okay, that sounds like fun."

I decided to take a chance.

She didn't show me any pictures of him, only that his name was Jacob.

"I want this to be a complete surprise for both of you and I don't want you to judge each other before you meet, so don't ask for any photos," she said. She was going to text him my number later.

The fact that she said *I don't want you to judge each other* made me think that he was going to be this closet weirdo that was obsessed with anime and played *RuneScape* all the time. But I thought this was a very interesting strategy on her part. I had never been set up to meet an actual stranger before. All I knew was his name . . . and I was intrigued.

About a day after meeting with Jessica, Jacob ended up texting me and introducing himself. We chatted briefly and then transitioned the conversation into how random this all is to be meeting through some stranger in each other's class.

It was fun texting him. I assumed he felt the same because he asked me to meet up with him a week later at a local coffee shop. When I agreed, I was with my friend, Lizzie. Lizzie immediately told me that I needed to be careful, especially since I was meeting a stranger.

We decided to do some investigating on Facebook, however, only knowing his first name created a big dilemma. We researched every boy with the name Jacob that was in a twenty-mile radius. We didn't stop at Jacob, we also searched for Jake, Jakob, Jaicub, and Jay; you'd be surprised how many spellings and nicknames a name can have.

Of course, as we browsed through each profile and photo, we weren't any closer to actually finding the right Jacob. It was time to cross my fingers and hope for the best.

(Side note: make sure to tell your family or friends where you are going on your first date. It's a best practice and you should always be safe, even if your date isn't a stranger! There are so many stories out there about missing girls, boys never coming home, or just fatal car accidents that can happen because it was dark outside or something crazy jumped out onto the road. Just please keep your loved ones informed.

Oh, and learn self defense or buy pepper spray. Now, I for one know that if a 200-pound man came after me I wouldn't make a dent on him if I started punching, but if I pulled out an eye gouge or pepper spray, I could save myself. Yes, this may sound like the longest public safety announcement ever, but I needed to say it.)

Meet Cute?

The day had come.

I was about forty minutes late to our blind date and I can honestly say it was because I had just installed a GPS navigator in my car. I was so technologically challenged that I didn't realize I had put in the wrong address. GPS technology for your vehicle had just come out and I felt like a fish out of water.

Finally, after circling the parking lot, I saw a boy in the corner of my rearview mirror sitting by himself on the outside patio of Local Coffee. I didn't see his face, only his frame. He wore a blue shirt, just like Jacob had told me he would be wearing.

I got out of my car, checked my teeth for leftover food, and flattened my hair down to try and look presentable. I was nervous. Luckily, my friends knew where I was and if anything were to have happened to me, Lord knows there would have been a reckoning.

I walked up the concrete steps to the main sidewalk that led to the Local Coffee patio. From a distance, I saw the boy looking down at his phone. He wore a blue shirt and khaki shorts. I walked toward him.

There was a bit of a breeze at that moment. In a way, I felt like it was carrying me towards him. I was nervous, but excited. Every step I took made my heart jump.

"Hi! Are you Jacob?" I smiled.

He looked up at me.

He was a beautiful, auburn-haired stranger looking like a poster child for a college football team. His eyes were the prettiest shade of green with a deep brown tint at the edge of his iris. I swear, the first time I met Jacob, I knew that he was going to be someone important in my life.

"I am. Hello, Isabella. Nice to finally meet you," he said and smiled back.

It was a great first date. We talked about our interests, rambled on about the foreign accents we could do, and walked around the shopping center for about six hours. But most importantly, he didn't kiss me.

I didn't believe in kissing on the first date. When I was younger, I did, and we all know exactly where those reckless kisses led me. Lucky for me, I had learned from my first experience of love to not put everything out there on the table, and since I also refused to give up my virginity in high school, I basically killed two birds with one stone in dating situations. If he can't wait then we can't date, plain and simple. I didn't get that vibe from Jacob though. He was sweet and kind. We could talk for hours about anything. I had never had this type of connection with someone so immediately before. We continued to talk every day after that night, and even when I went back to school in the fall, we made our communication work.

It was mid-fall, and the breeze of the night was impeccable—the type of weather that when you straighten your hair it doesn't frizz after five minutes. We had been on a couple of dates already and had decided to meet up to watch a free screening of the 90's classic film *Teenage Mutant Ninja Turtles*.

I sat on his lap on a bench in front of the movie theater. He asked me what my favorite movies were, and I responded with my go-to Disney classics and the *Rocky* series. He just laughed and told me I was cute.

About fifteen minutes before the movie started, I noticed the closeness of our faces. I knew that we probably should be heading inside, but I was determined to finally kiss him; there was also the slight chance that he could be just as shy as I was and not try to kiss me at all. At every word that came out of my mouth during the conversation, my mouth was slyly trying to get closer to his. He did the same.

It had been a while since I had kissed someone else. I forgot the feeling. Someone told me once that if you forgot what kissing felt like, just kiss the top of your hand. I will neither confirm nor deny that I practiced this once out of curiosity.

I looked up to see the speckled stars blanket across the night sky. The breeze was building so I leaned down to my oversized purse to grab my sweater. I put it on, and my goosebumps cleared immediately. When I looked up, I noticed that his eyes were set on mine. He looked at me, smiled intimately, and under his last breath he gently leaned in, grazing my lips with his touch—so soft. My stomach leaped as my lips fell into his. I have had my fair share of kisses, but this one was different. His lips were soft and comforting, fitting into the curve of my own perfectly, as if they were destined to touch. Nothing could truly describe that moment. It was perfect.

For the next few months, we spent every moment we could together, going to concerts, roller-skating in the park—he even let me drive his life-size Tonka Truck of a vehicle. This was a big deal because he treated his 2004 Chevy pickup like it was his baby. I thought I was in a monster truck show on the street. He would even surprise me with flowers and call me at numerous parts of the day *just because*. I felt so special.

Two days after Valentine's Day, and after a few months of dating, we decided to make s'mores in the backyard of his parents' house. He was still living with his parents at the time, so we were trying to keep quiet with our laughter. Every sentence was something funny—even the word *crackers* would have probably made me pee in my pants by how the mood was set. S'mores was such a great idea, especially when we added Reese's Peanut Butter Cups to the mix. In my mind, there is no better finger food on a date because if you get some on your face you can get it off with a sweet kiss, literally.

"Isabella, I have something to tell you . . ."

There I was, my fingers dripping with chocolate. My hair had magically stayed in place that night, as opposed to its usual Mufasa status, and I felt confident, even with my chocolate fingers. I could tell by his smile that he was enjoying this time with me and couldn't believe how connected we had become. Although it had only been a couple of months, I felt so close to him, more than any boy I had ever known.

Those past few months were something I had never experienced before; I felt comfort and adventure. We were technically in a somewhat long-distance relationship because my school was about a three-hour drive from him, but that didn't stop me.

When he said he had something to tell me, I felt in my heart that he was going to tell me he loved me. I loved him, too. That was the fastest feeling of love I had ever felt with someone, and it was incredibly intoxicating.

"Well, I think I have something to tell you, as well," I said.

I looked at him under the moonlight, swallowed my marshmallow whole, and looked back at him again, smiling as I wiped off my hands.

He looked at me and his eyes looked glassy. The fire from the pit cast a glimmer on his face, etching out his angled features and highlighted his auburn hair. I could see him biting the inside of his mouth while trying to make eye contact with me. When our eyes did meet, he looked down. I couldn't tell if he was blushing or not because of the fire's light. By that point, he was making me feel like something was wrong. I couldn't handle another broken heart. I was nervous.

I had finally gotten the chocolate off my fingers when he took my hand.

"I'm going to count down to three, okay. That way we both say what we want to say at the same time."

I nodded.

"One . . . two . . ."

My heart was pounding, and my eyes were widening with excitement. I felt like I was getting ready to dive into the deep end of a swimming pool. My mind, however, was wondering what he would say. If he wasn't going to say that he loved me, I would look like an idiot if I said that I loved him first.

"Three . . ."

We both stopped to look at each other and I held my breath because I wasn't sure if I should speak first or not.

"I love you," Jacob said.

There it was. Tears rolled down his eyes and I gently sighed in relief.

"I know I said I've been in love before, but I was wrong. You're everything to me," he said, wiping his eyes. "I love you, and I mean that."

"I love you, too," I said.

There was no pause in between. I knew I loved him. *This is what love is supposed to feel like.*

We cried in each other's arms and wouldn't let go. I finally caught myself laughing in his embrace because of how incredibly happy I was and how much of a movie scene this moment felt like. I couldn't believe this was happening to us—to me especially. Imagine, we were just a couple of strangers who happened to open each other's hearts at the same, perfect time.

This feeling was such an incredibly different feeling from my first love. I felt the emotion more intensely, to where I questioned if I even loved Anthony at all. Being with Jacob truly opened my eyes to a new feeling of love and lust at the same time. I had never experienced that before. The passion we had for each other was dangerous in an exciting way and I knew that all I wanted to do at that very moment was be with him.

After an intimate crying session, Jacob and I kissed intensely. We couldn't keep our hands off each other. I had never felt so connected to another human being in my life. *So this is what it feels like.* At that moment, everything seemed perfect. I wasn't scared one bit. I loved him and I trusted him.

Dead Butterflies

Almost a year into my relationship with Jacob, we decided to take the next step as boyfriend and girlfriend. It was a late night on the weekend and Jacob and I were alone in my apartment.

It was just another date night. Of course, I had thought about the possibility of sex actually happening between us, but I wasn't thinking too much about it. We had just finished watching *Baby Momma* and I slipped into my usual pajamas. He, on the other hand, was just in basketball shorts and a V-neck shirt. When he visited, we always slept in the same room, but with boundaries in place. Only this time, it was different.

After high school, there is this newfound freedom that overcomes you. It's this coming-of-age feeling where you're not fully on your own but feel liberated that your parents aren't across the hall checking in on you every five minutes anymore. It's a time when you are held fully accountable for all of your decisions, and when you learn what a mistake truly feels like.

That night, I gave Jacob my virginity and I cried. I cried so much. I was raised to believe that I should only be with one person my whole life, which should be my husband. Jacob had given his virginity to someone else before me in high school, so he wasn't as emotional as I was during that moment. However, I accepted that I had made this decision and loved him more than I had ever loved anyone before. Therefore, in my mind, I knew that he was going to be mine and I would be his forever.

He comforted me in every way he could, but I was so affected by what we did. I knew I couldn't go back. It was a moment that I knew felt right, but at the same time I felt guilty. And in my mind, I replayed the saying *what is lost is lost forever*. My body trembled as we laid there side by side. I was waiting for my guilt to go away, but it never did.

I loved him, but I wasn't fully happy with my decision. I wasn't his first and that itself was such an emotional process for me. But he was mine and I came to terms with that, knowing that he loved me just as much, or even more, than he had ever loved someone before me.

Monday morning came and I could not concentrate. Walking across campus, my mind was intoxicated by thoughts of him again—his feeling, his voice, his touch. He consumed my every thought. I have absolutely no idea how I managed to pass my finals later that week with him taking up all of my brain space.

Every text and call from him from then on exhilarated my soul. My happiness revolved around him, and I was all in. There was nothing I wouldn't have done for that boy, and I showed him that in every way I could.

The weekend before the upcoming fall semester, I decided to pack up my things again and drive to him and visit. Jacob rarely came up to see me, but I thought it was okay because I knew he had a lot going on at school and I wanted to be supportive.

Whenever I would see him, it was pure bliss. Neither one of us had a job at the time, but I used some of my college money to take us out to restaurants and movies on the weekends. It didn't bother me in the beginning because I knew we were both starting out and I always wanted to do nice things for him.

I spent all my weekends with him, so I never had much time to hang out with anyone else. The friends I made in my classes would ask me to hang out, but I always rejected their invitation because I couldn't give up my time with Jacob.

Two months before our one-year anniversary, he came to visit me. Everything seemed pretty normal. My roommate and I decided to go to one of the local parks and Jacob joined us. I noticed that he kept texting during our outing, but I never thought anything of it, at first.

"Jacob, who are you texting?" I asked during our stroll.

We had been at the park for no more than thirty minutes, and he was possessed by his phone. Just like any suspicious twenty-year-old girl would do, I took a glimpse at the name of who he was texting. Jennifer was the only thing I made out.

"She's a girl in my class back home. Don't worry, it's about school stuff. Besides, she's ugly and has a really big forehead."

A weird feeling immediately came over me.

"What does her being ugly have to do with anything?" I said, concerned. "Also, what is so important about school that you have to talk to her on a Saturday?"

He looked at me with his perfect eyes and said: "Don't worry, I love you. Why would I want to be with anyone else but you? You're crazy if you think anything is happening. I can have friends that are girls, right?"

I smiled crookedly and left it alone. He made me feel awful for questioning him. I was in a serious and sexual relationship now—someone who had taken my virginity would respect me no matter what. The whole point of being together was having that trust, right?

The next weekend came, and I was on cloud nine again driving down to see Jacob. His parents wouldn't be home that weekend, so I was filled with butterflies and was ready to be in the arms of the man that I was obsessed with.

When I arrived, everything was how it usually was. I wasn't particularly bothered with anything except that he was still texting someone late that night and I was not happy. I had a deep suspicion that it was that girl again, but I didn't look at his phone. Trust is something I needed to learn, so I went on with the night acting as normal as I could.

The next morning, I woke up next to him after a very cozy night's sleep. We had decided the day before that we were going to go out to the local grocery store and pick up a few items to make breakfast. Eggs, bacon, shredded cheese, and flour tortillas—a typical Tex-Mex breakfast.

"Good morning," he said and kissed me on my forehead.

I rolled over and yawned to wake myself up before I headed to the bathroom. We slept in until ten, which was a nice change to the early morning school schedule I kept during the weekdays.

After washing my face and finishing up my morning routine, I headed back into his room and noticed he wasn't there. I made my way down the stairs of his parent's house to find him taking out dishes from the dishwasher.

"Want to leave in about fifteen minutes to the grocery store?" he said.

"Of course. That gives me enough time to get ready," I replied.

I began to turn back to the other room and head up the staircase.

"Oh, Bella. Can you grab my phone for me? It's upstairs near my bed."

"You got it!"

I hurried up the stairs to get dressed and put on some makeup. I got my purse ready to go and looked up some recipes on Pinterest to see if there was anything extra we could pick up to make for dinner later.

Walking around his room to make sure I wasn't forgetting anything of mine, I glanced over at his bedside table where I saw his phone laying there.

"Oh yeah! I almost forgot," I said to myself.

As I held his phone in my hand, I remember having a gut feeling to look at his text messages. I didn't want to become the untrusting girlfriend, but I figured that if he said it was nothing then looking at his messages shouldn't be anything bothersome.

We had exchanged iPhone passcodes about a month or two before because he was always trying to get into my phone for my Pandora music account. My thoughts then were that it was only fair that if he had my iPhone passcode, then I should have his. He agreed.

As I lifted his phone, I felt such a weight of stress come over me. I was toying with the idea of being a bad girlfriend for snooping around. Although I validated my thoughts earlier about me unlocking his phone,

I still felt overpowered with guilt . . . that is, until I opened his phone.

When the screen unlocked, it immediately went to an open texting conversation that he was having. Not just any conversation to his mom or something, but to that girl in his class, Jennifer.

I saw that he had messaged her early that same morning about the time we woke up, telling her good morning and wondering what she was doing. Then I scrolled back to earlier messages—messages from the day before and throughout the week of me being gone. I soon found out that they have been seeing each other for a while and these messages proved it. They were talking about massaging each other, sending pictures, and coordinating when they would see each other after school. The worst part was that he was instigating everything and treating their friendship like a relationship.

As I kept scrolling and scrolling, the messages became too much for me.

Jennifer: *I want to see you again. That way we can finish what we started.*
Jacob: *I want you so bad. I'll meet up with you after this weekend.*

My heart went heavy. I felt furious, upset, heartbroken, ashamed, and used. I wanted to scream at the top of my lungs and fling everything on his desk out the window. I wanted to run away from him and go back to my apartment. I was disgusted.

As much as I wanted to do all those things at that very moment, I didn't. Instead, I took a few minutes to breathe and I grabbed all the items I had upstairs in his room and packed everything up. I went to the bathroom with no tears and fixed my hair and makeup. I was ready to face him.

My heart was racing, and I was filled with so much anger that I didn't even know how to control it. So, I took a deep breath, and made my way down the final step of his parent's staircase. I took another deep breath before placing both feet on the floor and then went straight to the kitchen.

There he was, walking in from the opposite end of the room with his jacket on and ready to head out to the grocery store, his keys in hand.

"What's wrong?" he said immediately.

He saw that I had all my bags packed, grasping his phone like I was about to throw it on the floor. I didn't, but I should have.

"How dare you," I said quietly, trying not to cry.

I looked directly at his puzzled face. He looked dumbfounded and his eyes seemed lost.

"You got a text message from Jennifer. Glad to see you texted her good morning, along with all the other interesting messages you've been sending her."

His eyes widened and he just stood there like a deer in the headlights.

"You've been spending time with her while I've been gone during the week. I have the proof," I screamed. "You totally slept with her!"

A migraine came over me and I was frustrated more than I can even describe. My body was tense, and my mind fixated on how much I wanted to punch him and scream. I felt disgusted and used.

I couldn't look at him, so I looked down at his phone in my hand and then threw it at him.

He dodged my throw and the phone fell to the ground with an audible crack. When he picked up the phone, he immediately started to cry—just like a baby. He tried to pull me into an embrace, smothering me with his arms while I pushed away, wanting to escape. His tears got all over my shirt and I was not having it.

"I'm so sorry. I never wanted to hurt you. I will never speak to her again. I'm so sorry. Can we forget this ever even happened?"

"The only reason you are crying is because you got caught. If I didn't go through your phone, you would still be talking to her and planning to see her this week. I had the biggest gut feeling and I was right," I yelled. I then stood back and took a deep breath.

"Did you have sex with her?"

No answer. I kept asking him repeatedly and then asked why he was cheating on me and for how long. He just kept crying and wouldn't give me a straight answer to anything. He repeatedly kept saying how sorry he was. I reminded him that we were in a sexual relationship and that I trusted him with my heart and my body. I did everything for him to try to make him happy.

"I let you touch me," I said, with tears coming down my face.

I slapped him right across the cheek. There was an echo of silence that followed.

He looked back at me again with tears. I was not going to feel sorry for him, and since he wasn't answering any of my questions, I decided to grab my things and bolt out of the house. Jacob followed me outside and tried to make me change my mind about leaving, but I left anyway. I couldn't look at him.

Catholic Guilt

I want to tell you I never saw him again. I want to tell you that after that day I didn't give in to anything he told me, no matter how many times he apologized. I want to tell you everything in my life was better after that day and that I was more confident with myself than ever—that I even managed to find happiness within myself. I want to tell you that I thrived even more in college and created so many memories. I want to tell you that I moved on. But I can't. And sadly, those words would be far from the truth.

After that day, I felt a tremendous guilt rush over me. Why? Because I beat myself up more than I like to admit. Catholic guilt is what I like to call this portion of my life.

Although I was angry and hurt by him about what he did, I was still in love with him. It was confusing to me because you would think that once someone goes behind your back and cheats that you should never want anything to do with them. Well, that didn't happen to me.

Unfortunately, he kept calling me and telling me he was sorry, and it turned into me begging him to stay with me. It got to a point where

I was suddenly the one to blame and he managed to dangle my heart with puppet strings. I remember that night I was crying more about the thought of him leaving me than him actually being with another woman. It was more about me thinking about my virginity. I was afraid of sleeping with someone else since I made a promise to myself that if I were to lose my virginity to someone before I was married, that I would only sleep with that person, so it would be as if I had truly only given myself to one man for the rest of my life. This is where the Catholic guilt came into play and holds a big piece as to why I ended up putting up with so much later on.

For all you Catholic girls and boys out there, you are taught early how precious your body is. I remember going to one of my youth group sessions one Sunday and discussing the book *Theology of the Body* by Christopher West and the importance of waiting for marriage before having sex. This was also right before college, so it was very insightful. I remember them giving us a journal to write to our future spouses to let them know how much we valued ourselves and would wait for their true love. I still believed this teaching, which made everything much more heartbreaking.

Eventually Jacob and I made up, but this time there was a shift in power. Instead of being strong willed, my confidence was shot, and I was afraid of doing anything that might make him stray. We had no trust between one another, and he made it clear that he was the one who made the decision to get back together. I saw how he fed off of the desperate compliments I would give him regarding his body, love, and how much I needed him. At that point, I was saying anything to make sure he was satisfied with me so that we could make everything between us be what it once was, but better. But the truth was, I wasn't the only one lacking confidence; I saw that he was becoming insecure himself.

Have you ever been in a relationship with no trust? It's awful. Every day is like a mind game because you play roulette against yourself, and the odds you face always result in a loss. I was always losing because I never truly got over his lies and what he did behind my back, and living in different cities cut me to the core because I knew there was nothing I could do to stop whatever he decided to do without me.

It sounds crazy now as I reflect on everything, but I remember having a little panic attack every day during that school semester because my mind kept wandering to the idea of him going back to school and meeting another girl in his class. That was how he had met the other woman, so I naturally became obsessed with asking about his day and calling him every one to two hours. The school semester lasted about four months, so my anxiety skyrocketed during that time, and my insecurity did the same.

To cope with my anxiety, I started to run. I ran around campus, on the treadmills at the campus gym, and all around the city parks to release my thoughts. Although this did wonders for my mental health and wellness, it was a temporary fix. After I'd shower, I'd lay in my room reading for class, unable to focus on my studies because my mind was consumed by him. I remember going to my doctor and telling her that I kept having migraines and my body kept hurting, even after I would stretch following my workouts.

She told me I had hypertension in my back and recommended an MRI, just in case there might be a serious reason causing my sudden migraines. She also recommended I should see a therapist to make sure I wasn't going into depression. By the grace of God, they didn't find anything serious that could be causing my migraines.

"Maybe you're just really stressed out?" the MRI technician said to me when the exam was complete.

When I got migraines after that, I blamed it on stress. I tried to seek a therapist, but the wait was either too long or their sessions wouldn't fit my school schedule. I decided to push forward anyway.

Growing Pains

I viewed our first year together as an accomplishment; we managed to stay together, and he still said he loved me. This was my longest relationship ever at that point, and I was ready to see how everything would unfold. In my mind, if we had made it through all that crap so far, we could conquer anything. However, this hopefulness wouldn't last long.

Jacob kept making excuses not to come up to visit me because he didn't want to drive, so he tended to guilt-trip me into driving to him every weekend. I would bail on my roommate and the few friends that I did have just to make an effort to accommodate.

It was always the same routine: eat, sleep, and watch a movie. He then started getting into the habit of smoking weed. He said he needed it due to his anxiety because of school. I was in my junior year at my university, and he was still considered a sophomore at the local community college. Say what you want about community colleges, they are a great resource for saving money, but if you do not take classes seriously and become indecisive with your future then you have a problem. Jacob had this problem.

He would talk and talk about everything he wanted to do in life. He had big dreams and was ambitious in his own way. However, when it came to actually doing something about it, he would fail to do any of the work. For example, he would skip class on purpose because he didn't *feel good* that day. I'd like to consider myself a mental health advocate for all, but when you are with someone who consistently uses the same excuses to get out of something difficult, it becomes frustrating. While I would study around him, he would choose to play video games. I did try to encourage him in any way I could, but a girlfriend can only do so much. Now, I'm not going to bash the man to smithereens, but I will say I had to be very careful not to ruin his ego. Like everyone, I had dreams, too, and was doing everything I could to try and accomplish them.

My dream of journalism stayed with me into my college years. Writing is one of my passions, and I was a bright-eyed twenty-one-year-old at the time just trying to get something started. Walking through campus, I would see the university newspaper available at every corner. It gave me the idea that I should try and see if I could get a spot on the news staff. I marched myself into their newsroom that day to see if I could speak to somebody about applying for a position.

"You're in luck," one of the student editors told me. "We're looking for writers. We have a few prompts we ask applicants to write about. From there, we determine who would be best to fill our positions. We'll contact you if you get selected."

Challenge accepted.

I was giddy at the idea of even having the opportunity to write for the campus newspaper; that would be such a dream. I immediately texted Jacob about it. He seemed as excited as someone could be over a text message, but all in all, he received my news positively.

"Let's see how you do," he texted me.

That night, I was up with my roommate until about midnight. I was in the zone, brainstorming ideas to fulfill their prompts and outlining ways to execute them. I loved that I would be judged by my talent alone and I felt this would be a great opportunity to see what I could do. My passion was igniting.

The next day after completing my studies, I started to flesh out my two best outlines. It took me about seven hours to finish both prompts because I was taking a fine editing comb through my work to make sure I wasn't misspelling anything. I then submitted both pieces later that week.

I didn't speak with Jacob much that week. He knew I was really trying hard to submit some good work, so when I would speak to him on the phone it would only be for a couple of minutes. He was still my priority in his mind but having the opportunity to be a part of something that fulfilled my passion was a whole new experience for me.

Two weeks later, I received an email from the university newspaper. When I opened the email on my phone, I said a quick prayer and began to dive in. They liked my work and wanted to bring me on staff as a writer and editor for campus news.

I was over the moon. I let out a satisfying *yes*! in the campus courtyard and I was smiling ear to ear. That was the best day of my college career to that point, and I knew that moments like that didn't come very often. I was pleased with this opportunity and was ready.

"Jacob, I got offered a position on staff! They liked my work," I said over the phone.

There was silence on his end for a while. "I'm happy for you," he finally said.

It wasn't the enthusiasm I was looking for, but I didn't care. I felt accomplished and validated that my work was good enough—that I was good enough. It meant so much to me.

"We are supposed to have orientation next week to go over staff expectations and schedules. I'll keep you informed," I said.

"Okay," he quickly replied.

When orientation finally came, I was extremely giddy and full of excitement. Walking through the *staff only* entrance felt like I was walking on cloud nine and I couldn't wait to fully see the workspace.

I met so many people—writers, editors, and newbies like myself. I made a point to talk to the campus professors running the program, as well as the editor-in-chief. And as I began to chat with so many others,

I felt completely in the zone in what I felt would be the next chapter in my college life.

During the orientation, they stated that we had a staff meeting every Sunday morning to discuss projects and assignment topics. As soon as she said that, I immediately thought of Jacob. I had no problem staying up here every weekend. I never had a chance to while I'd been dating Jacob, and I felt this would be a good opportunity to change the direction of our relationship into accommodating my schedule for a change. That night when I went home, I spoke to Jacob over the phone to give him the update.

"So, I'm going to have to stay up here every weekend. Turns out, our staff meetings occur every Sunday and I don't want to jeopardize my standing with the staff."

"But what about us?" he responded immediately. "We're never going to see each other now that you have all this newfound responsibility. I love seeing you. I just don't know how we're going to make it through this."

My mouth dropped and my heart dropped even further. *Was he serious right now?*

"Jacob, I will still be able to see you. Maybe you can start coming up here more often? And when I come to see you, I can leave early in the morning on Sundays and things can totally work out. This opportunity is just really important to me, and I don't want to give it up."

An uncomfortable silence filled the call, and I could tell he was frustrated.

"I just think this is going to be bad for us. I want us to be together and I don't want anything to get in the way of that," he whined.

That whole week Jacob's comments consumed my brain again. My migraines came back because I was stressed at the idea of jeopardizing our relationship. I didn't want to tell my parents because I didn't want them to hate Jacob, so I talked to my roommate about it.

"Bella, you need to stay put with these meetings. You were so excited about this opportunity and now you want to throw it away because of your boyfriend?" she said.

She was so right, but my heart was still confused. Every night leading up to that first Sunday, I would pray to God and ask him to give me the strength to make the right decision. In the back of my mind, I knew I needed to follow through with this opportunity—but Jacob would be upset, and I didn't want to do that to him.

Every time we talked, he would bring up again and again how much this would affect our relationship and how he didn't think we would be able to stay together.

I had to make a choice.

Sunday morning came and I didn't show up to the news meeting.

I withdrew myself from being an editor on staff by email and told them that I was too busy with schoolwork at the time to really put in a 100 percent effort. A lie, it was all a lie. And I remember Jacob hugging me after I decided to give up on that opportunity.

"Thank you, Isabella. Thank you," he said.

My eyes were empty. Jacob couldn't care less because he was beaming. As soon as I saw how happy he was, I felt a little at ease with my decision, but I also knew what I had done was completely wrong.

Don't feel sorry for me, though. It was my decision and the fact that I was desperate to be with him proved that I was weak. However, something changed in me that day. I remembered driving back to my apartment and heading straight to my room. I didn't cry, but I read. I read my journal entries from the past week and my written words of excitement as I was given the opportunity to challenge myself in my writings. I reflected on what that opportunity meant to me, realizing that those emotions were valid less than a week ago. I also read my commentary about Jacob's behavior and how disinterested he was in the idea of me leaving him on Sundays.

Line by line, my migraines increased as I read deeper into the pages. I began to read the highlights of our relationship out loud to feel my very own words. It was all the proof I needed to show me I had made a mistake and I was finally listening to myself. From there, I decided to go back to previous entries and relive the awful days of his cheating and lies. I kept reading and reading, until I had to stop myself. I took a deep breath and began to search for the next available blank page to write on.

I wrote every detail of my feelings that day and would continue to do this for years. That day, I told myself that I would never give up my dreams for someone else again, even if I loved them.

The next year had its ups, but definitely had its downs. I decided to seek internship opportunities to help further my college resume, as well as find some friends to hang out with. Every day was something new with Jacob, whether he was upset that I didn't answer my phone immediately when he called, or that he was bothered when I wanted to see a friend after school to hang out.

Along with him making me feel bad for hanging out with other people, Jacob also lost his temper with me multiple times. One time, he found out that one of his friends thought I was pretty, and he punched a hole in the door of his room at his parent's house. You would think that would make me run, right?

To distract myself from his immaturity, I decided to keep myself busier than I had ever been before. I joined another organization in college to network, focused on my studies, and was passing my classes with flying colors. I began to build my resume as any college student would with my internships. Jacob was still at his community college and kept changing his major to a point where he had no plan as to what to do next. Still, I stayed with him and tried to make him feel okay throughout his educational experience.

Because he also wasn't working still, I was paying for everything on the weekends and proofread his homework during the late nights of the school week to help him out in any way I could. Although there were a lot of rough spots in our relationship, I was trying my hardest to stay content with who we were as a couple. But in the back of my mind, I was afraid of what post-graduation would look like.

Changes

Flash forward to my college graduation night. My whole family came up to join me for my graduation ceremony. It was such a happy day for us all. I was officially the first person in my family to graduate from a university. Seeing the looks on my parents' faces was priceless. My *abuelita* smiled from ear to ear seeing me walk toward her after the ceremony was over.

This was the greatest accomplishment of my life at that point. After years of studying, researching how to survive college, and applying myself to strive for more, I did it. It felt amazing. It was a dream I had always pictured in my mind and now it was finally my reality. There was nothing anyone could tell me that I couldn't do.

My *abuelita* was in tears hugging me, my parents and siblings were bombarding me with photos and flowers, and my degree was secured away. I had accomplished what I wanted and was looking forward to the future. Words cannot describe the joy I saw radiate from my mom and dad. Everyone was elated. Everyone, except Jacob.

I remember late that night before heading out to my graduation celebration downtown, Jacob and I decided to sit on the rooftop of my apartment complex while our friends were getting ready for the night. I noticed he had been distant that whole day, so I brought it up in conversation as we were looking up at the moon.

"You graduated so much faster than me. How do you think this all makes me feel?" Jacob said. "Now I just feel like a loser."

I tried to comfort him, but it was difficult for me because everything I kept saying to him had been what I'd been saying to him all along during the past two years of dating: *You got this. Keep studying and don't skip class. You'll do better next time. Don't give up.*

There was only so much I could do and say.

After that night, my mental state completely shifted. I kept replaying the words he said to me and how much jealousy he held toward me after graduation. I felt let down, unappreciated, but most importantly, unapologetic. I didn't feel sorry for him one bit because I had worked my butt off for this moment—and he took my moment away by being selfish.

This would continue for the next three years. *Yeah, you read that right.* Three years of him still not getting his degree, not finding a stable job, and complaining to me how he felt awful because of my success—and I held on because I felt like I had to.

There goes that Catholic guilt again. How could I leave the man when I had given him so much of myself already? I didn't want to waste the time that we'd spent together by throwing it all away. In my mind, it was a safe choice to just keep holding on.

I landed my first job three months after graduation and a year later I got accepted into a master's program at a local university to be closer to him. I wanted to venture out and leave Texas with every inch of my soul, but his sorrow and lackluster spirit felt superglued to my body. I couldn't leave him.

During my graduate program, he was still at the community college in town. He would take mental jabs at me weekly, saying that I wasn't *the girl of his dreams*, and would comment on my appearance here and there. Of course, whenever I would resurface his harsh words, he would deny any recollection of it and quickly try to snuggle up to me for another intimate moment.

When I graduated with my master's degree, I thought he wanted to disappear from the face of the earth. I didn't invite him to my graduation ceremony because he told me he wouldn't feel comfortable around my family. I personally didn't want him there either because my parents didn't like him, and I knew that what we had was something they did not want me to continue. He wasn't a fan of my younger sister and never made an effort to get to know my brothers, which was a huge red flag that hurt me immensely. The biggest red flag of them all was that my *abuelita* didn't like him—and my *abuelita* likes everyone.

Can you imagine being with someone who didn't feel comfortable with your success? Or worse, who was uncomfortable with your family? I felt like he was the worst-kept secret of my life during our time together when I was at any family gathering. I never mentioned him around my family, nor did they try to bring him up in conversation. The only one who ever mentioned him was my dad, who asked here and there if he had found a job yet or if he was ever going to stop by the house one day to say hello to the family. Of course, my response to both of those questions was "soon." But the day never came.

As I had mentioned before, my family means the world to me—they are what drives me every day. And to be placed in a position where the man that supposedly loved me did not want to make an effort to get to know the people who had raised me was heartbreaking. It was awful and his actions continued to take a toll on my mentality.

That summer, I had an opportunity to travel to Spain with some friends. My parents were all for me going and my friends had fired me up to go on an adventure. I decided to put in my two-weeks notice at my job at the time, exchange my money for euros, and move forward in booking my trip to Spain to explore. When I finally decided to tell Jacob, everything was already booked and paid for. He was not happy.

"You're going to meet someone over there. You're just going to leave me, I know it," he said.

Those were his initial thoughts when I shared my exciting news, but at this point I didn't care. I didn't expect him to be excited for me, which is sad to think about. It wasn't my fault he automatically defaulted to insecurity because of his actions while he'd been dating me. Of course, a part of me always felt bad for him, and I hated it.

After the ridiculous encounter I had with Jacob, I left for Spain and experienced some of the most beautiful parts of the world. I learned to salsa dance with my friends, met other young professionals from across the globe, ate eight-course meals almost every evening, drank the most incredible Spanish wine, and lived my life to the fullest with no one to question my actions. I rediscovered myself and my confidence in Spain and it was the best decision of my life to go.

Upon my arrival back to the States, I booked trips to Chicago and Las Vegas to expand my hunger for adventure. I spent more time with family and friends than I ever had before. I used my newfound freedom to enjoy my life and map out my next career and personal moves.

Jacob and I were still together, but I wasn't seeing him often. From my understanding, he was just staying home, getting high, and playing video games by himself. To this day, I'll never truly know what he was up to while I was gone. But I began to care less and less as time flew by.

About a month after I came back from Vegas with my girlfriends, Jacob and I were approaching our fifth anniversary of being together and I just couldn't take it anymore. I remember being at his parents' house one evening with his family just hanging out. His family was so wonderful and welcoming that I truly enjoyed being around them—but when Jacob entered the room, my mood would always sink.

"Are you excited that your anniversary is coming up again soon?" one of his sisters cheerfully asked me in passing.

Time seemed to stop after she spoke those words. I felt overwhelmed with sadness and confusion. I couldn't hold back my tears. I just looked at her, distraught. His sister was so kind and immediately pulled me into the guest bathroom and started to wipe my tears with Kleenex. She locked the door.

"What's wrong?" she said as she gave me a warm embrace.

She was the comfort I didn't know I needed. I told her about what a struggle the last few years had been and how sad I had become. I told her how I felt the need to move on, but that the guilt tying me to her brother for all those years had kept me from doing so. I told her how tired I was of being mistreated and discouraged, how I felt free being away from him for so long that summer. She hugged me close and looked me straight in the eyes.

"Look out for yourself and do what is right for you. I would have never guessed the struggle it has been, but thank you for trusting me," she said. "I won't tell a soul, but know that whatever decision you make, we will always care for you as a family."

I'll never forget her kindness.

I'd like to consider myself a very nice and polite person, but even nice people have their limits. For me, I guess it was five years. Everything he did—his laziness, how I had to pay for everything, his complaints, his lack of drive, even the way he chewed—just bugged me to the point that I did not care to be with him.

On our very last date, we went to the batting cages. He had annoyed me once again because he didn't have money, so I had to pay for lunch and the whole batting cage experience. He kept talking to this one guy in line about how he loves to play baseball, is studying to be a software engineer, and how he used to be an all-star lacrosse player in high school. I just rolled my eyes.

The boy was all talk and all he had to brag about was his athletic ability in high school. Regarding those software engineer dreams, he'd had many years of school to finish and wasn't even close.

I was mad—mad because it had taken me this long to realize how much I had put up with and to see the light. I wanted absolutely nothing to do with him. Words cannot describe how much of a light switch feeling it was for me to let go, mentally and physically.

When we left the batting cages, I drove us back to his parents' house. I told him that it was over and that I couldn't be with him anymore. He was distraught and cried and accused me of never truly loving him. He told me he was going to kill himself and that he was planning to propose to me and that I ruined everything. On the contrary, he had used those words against me for years to make me stay. Of course, as a young twenty-something, the fear of your boyfriend threatening to kill himself takes a huge toll on your mental health. They lure you in by putting guilt on your shoulders and accusing you of being the problem. This time, however, I just let him talk. Once he was done, I just looked at him without shedding a single tear and drove away.

This was such a significant moment for me because I cry about everything—*and I mean everything!* But when I don't, especially for big moments in my life, that truly means something. More specifically, it means that I don't care. Enough years had passed, and I had learned my lesson.

After our breakup, Jacob tried to meet up with me a few times in the course of two weeks. I was vulnerable, so I gave in once because I ultimately felt bad, but I shouldn't have. We went to dinner, he barely talked, and at the end of the night I asked for two separate checks because I wasn't going to pay for his meal again. He moped and wallowed around instead of trying to fight back for me.

He ended up following me to my car and sitting in the passenger's seat so we could talk. I was so disinterested that I could not even tell you what we talked about, just that I knew I was mentally done.

"Isabella, can I kiss you?" he said to me in the car.

He leaned it. Hesitantly, I kissed him back. And I felt nothing.

It was pleasurable, but there was nothing that he could do to change my mind otherwise. I know he had hope, but I had hope for almost five years, and nothing happened. He had tears in his eyes, and I gave him a big hug.

"You never loved me, did you? You just toyed with my emotions!" he said to me.

I took a deep breath.

"Jacob, I loved you so much. You were everything to me and I wanted my life to be with you. But now after going through so much, I realized there is a difference between loving someone and being in love with someone," I said. "I love you as a person, but I am no longer in love with you."

That was the unvarnished truth.

I never saw him after that day. He would try to contact me a few times after that meeting—one time he even called me eleven times on a random Saturday night because he was paranoid that I was sleeping with someone else already. He tried to meet up with me several times again, but I never even gave him the time of day. It wouldn't have been fair to give him hope where there was none to begin with. He was my most difficult relationship yet. Deep inside he truly is a good person, but he was not the right person for me.

What a feeling it was to finally be free! I'm not going to lie; I had a few weak moments where I was feeling guilty about the way I had ended things. So, to ease that weakness, I decided to call up my best friends and make plans for the coming weekends. The old me would have called him to see how he was doing, the new me was going to spend some quality time with my best friends. This was the fun part of the breakup. On top of feeling like myself again, my career was top of mind, and I knew my next career move would be somewhere far away from Texas. I was enjoying the weight lifted from my life and couldn't believe how long it had been since I was happy.

Here's a fun fact about this situation. As you know, I used to get migraines all the time when Jacob and I were together—literally almost every day. As soon as I left him, I have been migraine-free ever since.

Now, before anyone thinks I'm being too cynical about all of this, I want to say that I never wished any ill will toward him. I truly hoped that by me leaving him he would have the opportunity to reevaluate his life and the choices he had made about his career and his attitude toward women.

I don't regret my time with Jacob. Do I regret my personal, financial, and emotional investment with him? I mean, sometimes I get salty. But there was a certain moment in time that I wanted every ounce of him, and I can't deny that our form of love taught me a lot. I also really grew during my time with him, and I am thankful for the once-in-a-lifetime experiences I had with him and his family.

Another thing I learned was that in a relationship, love isn't enough. There needs to be trust, morals, a financial balance, and a friendship to keep the relationship strong. To add to this, you also need to like the person. Sure, you can love them, but do you like them? To like someone is to enjoy them for who they are—their presence, personality, sense of humor, and spirit. If you love them, but don't like them, that's a problem.

But let's dig a little deeper. I gave this boy everything from my body to my finances because I trusted him. Deep in my heart, I wanted to marry him, even with all his edges and flaws—but I knew it was all wrong. My mistake was putting too much trust into someone that didn't deserve it. I felt obligated to him because I gave him my virginity, but I lost more than just that. I lost my self respect, my courage, and my faith.

Did you notice that I rarely mentioned God and my faith during my time with Jacob? It would take some time for me to realize that not only was my relationship with Jacob keeping me away from my true self but hindering my relationship with God. As much as I wanted Jacob to join me at church or pray with me, he was never willing to try it. I'm not one to shove religion down someone's throat, but when it comes down to morals and spiritual beliefs in a serious relationship it's important. Besides, if you're with someone who resists the growth you seek in life, it's hard to create a strong foundation.

How was I supposed to know, right? How is anyone supposed to know? When you're young, you get high off the euphoria of someone saying that they love you. But love is more than just words and touch, it's actions. Maya Angelou said once that "when someone shows you who they are, believe them." All you can pray for is that your judgment of character will fall into place once their true identity is revealed.

Let me share with you one of the rawest lessons of my life: don't give your body and heart to just anyone. I believe that the reason I put up with so much from Jacob and continued to sympathize with him for years was because I gave him my virginity, the most vulnerable part of me at the time. Because of this, I felt that I subconsciously belonged to him, and it took me years to realize that this was absolutely not true. Regardless of your religion, take time to value your mind, body, and soul. You don't belong to anyone.

And for those who have had their body shared without consent—I hear you and I'm with you. Stories like yours are personal and sadly are too common. But to shine a light on this, nothing anyone does to your body defines your self worth. God doesn't love you any less and how you move forward is the blessing of grace.

For those of you like me who felt that they let themselves go by giving something precious to someone who didn't deserve it—you're still special. Nothing can take away your value as a person, but you have to fight for your worth and acknowledge your past so that you can move forward. Be strong with your morals and learn to love yourself before giving consent to someone else. Your body and mind are beautiful and precious, so don't let anyone make you feel hostage in your own skin.

❀❀❀

I close my laptop. There is a hint of sun at the far end of my living room. The light is coming in after such a cold weekend. I need some time to breathe and soak everything in—all of these experiences that had shaped me. Nothing about placing your thoughts on paper is easy, especially when you want to share them with the world.

I change quickly into some jogging sweats and a long t-shirt. I wrap my hair in a low ponytail and connect my air pods to my phone. I need to release myself again. Reliving that chapter was difficult, but necessary.

After a few yoga stretches, I go for a long run.

Goodbye, Friend

Two months after my breakup with Jacob, I was offered a job in New York and had a month before my big move. I was also invited to a post-Christmas party at an old high-school friend's house and felt it would be nice to see old friends before I left. I went alone since I hadn't really kept in touch with too many people from my hometown. I did know a few people who were going to be there that I was texting beforehand, so that kept me at ease and I felt okay walking up to the front porch.

As soon as I knocked on the door, I was immediately greeted by my old high school friend, Sebastian, and was embraced with a giant hug. Like clockwork, I immediately felt a gutted feeling in my stomach because my heart felt what my mind was already suspecting.

There, in the far back of the house, was Anthony, staring at me from across the room with his friends and a group of girls surrounding him. I, on the other hand, didn't look his way at all and model-walked straight to the bathroom before making my entrance back into the living room to mingle. I kept my cool—or at least I tried to.

It was nice seeing the faces of so many people I used to know. Jacob kept messaging me and calling me left and right asking to see me. I just ignored my phone.

Have you ever felt the eyes of someone watching you? Like no matter where you went, you felt this beaming energy upon you? Well, that was Anthony. I could feel him, even though we were several feet away from each other. It's like having butterflies, but with edgy excitement. The best way I could describe this feeling was like I was seconds away from a roller coaster drop I knew was coming.

I came out of the bathroom at one point of the night and passed a grown-up Caleb walking up to talk to me. I was genuinely happy to see him—after so many years, it was refreshing to see another familiar face. Of course, as soon as I gave Caleb a hug, Anthony was right behind him staring at me.

I took a deep breath, locked eyes with him, and gave him the biggest smile. As soon as I let go of my embrace with Caleb, I walked towards Anthony and gave him the biggest hug. It felt like old times.

The three of us talked about life, our current plans, and how Anthony and I ultimately did end up going to rival schools for college. But of course, like any good catch up, we began to talk about love.

"I don't believe in having a relationship so early in your twenties," Anthony said. "It's your time to be young and experience life."

"I completely disagree. You should date throughout your twenties and have relationships, especially if the person is amazing," Caleb said.

"What about you, Bella? What do you think?" Caleb asked as Anthony's eyes closed in on mine.

I took a deep breath and smirked.

"I actually agree with Anthony on this one," I said. "I believe that we are young, and we should take advantage of being selfish with our time and focus on ourselves. But if you find someone that is worth it—like really worth it—then you should take a chance on a relationship."

I smiled at Caleb and felt Anthony's eyes upon me again.

"Are you dating anyone, Bella?" Anthony asked while sipping from his red solo cup.

"No," I said. His eyes widened.

A few girls then came up and started grabbing onto Anthony. I just left the space and looked for some water. Toward the end of the night, I realized how late it was, and I didn't want to drive past midnight. I decided to grab my things and head home to end the night. I said goodbye to some old friends and noticed Caleb sitting on the edge of the sofa.

"Isabella, are you leaving?" Caleb said.

I started chatting with Caleb about how great it was seeing each other but noticed that Anthony was standing not even a foot away from us, looking directly at me while the girls who were grabbing onto him earlier were trying to distract him.

There was a moment when I caught a bit of Anthony's conversation with one of the girls.

"Who is that girl to you, Tony?" said one of the girls.

I knew she was talking about me because his stare was constant during my conversation with Caleb.

"She was my first love," he said.

A smile came over me.

I then stopped chatting with Caleb and turned to my left to look at Anthony directly in the eye again. As I walked toward him, his stare remained constant, and I opened my arms to give him the biggest hug.

"It was great catching up with you tonight," I whispered in his ear. "Good luck with everything."

I left his embrace and looked up at his face, only to see him speechless with his blue eyes staring right back at mine, just like they used to. I smiled, turned around, and walked away. He didn't know I heard his words, but I hope he felt my gratitude with my embrace.

I never saw Anthony again or spoke to him after that day. It's for the best; we both needed to move on with our lives and were on different paths. But being able to see each other once more and relive the butterflies was a nice reminder of the past. I believe this was a God thing, truly. And the final words he spoke aloud, not realizing that I heard them all, was the reassurance I needed that I was just as special to him as he was to me. It gave me the closure I needed to let go of after all those years. He was the first boy to touch my heart, the last boy I could ever forget, and the only boy that could have ever helped me move forward.

Three

So This Is Love

When I was a little girl, I would dream about finding my Prince Charming. I had the perfect scenario: we would get engaged in front of Cinderella's castle at Disneyworld and then walk inside Cinderella's ballroom and get married immediately afterward. I would have the same ball gown as Belle from *Beauty and the Beast* and be surrounded by glass windows overlooking the ocean. I wanted to be a princess so badly and live happily ever after with the perfect man. But when I grew up, still hopeful that fairytales can come true, my mind started to dream bigger. I'd dream about going to a big university, becoming the editor-in-chief of *Time* magazine, and meeting Britney Spears. And if I was really lucky, I would make my mark in the world like Selena Quintanilla-Perez.

When I would tell my parents my dreams, they would try to persuade me to do something else. I broke my dad's heart when I told him I didn't want to go into the medical field. He simply warned me of how much struggle I was going to face since my dreams weren't *practical* in their minds. I think every child, especially first or second-generation children of immigrants, gets bopped in the head with the idea that you must be a doctor or lawyer to be considered successful. I, on the other hand, was looking for another route to success. They had every right to feel that way—especially because they didn't want me to struggle like they did. But in my heart, I knew my fate was going to be different and I was determined to prove myself.

Putting yourself out there is tough, especially when you're trying to achieve your dream. People along the way may tear you down, reject your spirit, or judge you by your appearance. I remember speaking with the parents of one of my friends about my dream school one day at their house. Their mother literally told me that it would be impossible for me to go to my dream school—and then look at what happened.

No one can take away your accomplishments or your kindness. And if you get really lucky, you will find someone who embraces both your heart and your mind. Remember how I referenced early on in these writings about finding your third love, the one that just feels right? Well, hear me out, because I have a few thoughts about this.

I think the mindset of your third love being perfect is a wonderful thought, but I think that it goes deeper than that. I feel that when you find your third big love is when you are also on the road to loving yourself. I think you need to grow up, experience life, accomplish your goals, and stop searching for a fairytale, and let everything find you when you least expect it.

With Anthony, I was a child learning things day by day and trying to keep up with the idea of being in love. With Jacob, all I was trying to do was stay afloat—learning the value of faith and hard work the hard way because nothing is possible without them both. Dealing with prejudice was an eye opener for me. It tested the confidence I had within myself and the respect I had for others. I could have given up on humanity in general, but didn't, and I grew with the mindset of kindness and how essential it is. I had to lose myself to love myself. I feel like I am growing into my third love and learning to love myself along the way. And learning to love myself will allow me to fall in love with the right person.

And just like that, God sent me Adam.

Adam is love. The most beautiful and genuine love that I have ever known. He is kind, smart, handsome, and is the funniest man I know. I can go on and on about this beautiful man, but I won't—some things are best kept private. Private in the way that shows respect and love for him because the way he loves me helped me realize that true love does exist.

I have never felt more secure and encouraged in a relationship in my life. When he tells me I'm smart and beautiful, I believe him—every inch of my soul believes him. Another incredible aspect of our relationship is that he loves God just like me. We go to church together and pray for each other. I know now that's what I needed and missed in previous relationships.

I remember freaking out at the start of our relationship. Adam was being so nice and thoughtful to me that I anticipated his actions to be fake since my traumatizing experience with Jacob started the same way and turned into a disaster. But I wasn't going to let a man from my past ruin my future. After two years of Adam being respectful, thoughtful, not jealous, and just an overall protector, it was very clear to me that he is good. *So very good.*

My relationship with God has grown during our time together, as well as my confidence. I'm able to spend time with my friends without jealousy, and Adam and I are focused on our careers while prioritizing our love for one another. After the first six months of dating him, I remember writing in my journal and reflecting on how different it was to be in a healthy relationship. Because I was so traumatized from my past, accepting Adam's genuine feelings for me took a little while to get used to. But along the way, Adam helped me feel secure in our relationship and in my own skin.

Now don't get me wrong, our relationship isn't perfect. But our foundation is strong because of our faith and how much we accept each other's pasts and present. We are complete opposites, but are both adventurous, spirited, and each other's biggest cheerleaders. We treat each other with respect and embrace each other's background and cultures— not to mention my parents and siblings absolutely adore him! He makes me feel like I'm home, even when I'm so far away from home right now.

Moving to New York for a great job opportunity, my life felt like it was finally coming together. Throughout this journey, I was able to find more pieces of myself and began to love the person I was becoming while I was growing in love with Adam. Although I didn't need Adam to show me who I was and what I was capable of, he became the support I didn't know I needed to give me the reassurance of how worthy I was of the blessings in my life.

He challenges me in the best way and helps me understand the important things in life: faith, family, fun, and forgiveness. I learned that forgiving myself and forgiving others was the only way I could move forward in my life—which has brought me to where I am today.

Another big factor in this growth was learning to listen to God again. My gut feelings and moments in tears were the hints God would place along my path for me to see. Now, sometimes it took a lot longer for me to get over those hurdles, but it was ultimately all in God's timing. Do I regret the decisions of my past? At first I did, but now I do not.

Although there are areas in my previous relationships where I wish I could have smacked myself with a Bible, I now realize that everything happened the way it was intended to.

At the start of my relationship with Adam, I remember my friends telling me "See, look how happy you are! You should have broken up with Jacob a long time ago . . ."

There's a problem with that statement: if I had broken up with Jacob a few years earlier and skipped the drama, who knows if Adam and I would have met at all? I'm telling you, if it wasn't for the exact moment in time that things happened the way they did, Adam and I wouldn't have ever crossed paths. It's truly fascinating when you piece everything together.

I'm not a preacher or a pastor, or even a psychologist for that matter, but I am a woman of faith. I am human and I think the biggest lesson to take away from these instances is that sometimes you have to live through the motions in order to understand what you don't want in life. It took me years to finally make decisions for myself but finding that strength and having faith will lead you in the right direction.

I don't know what's going to happen with me and Adam. But I know whatever happens, it's going to be special. Life is fascinating; one day you're a teenager feeling like your life is over because your heart is broken for the first time, and the next day you're accomplishing your goals and falling in love with the right man.

You don't go looking for love, it finds you—at least that's what my experience with God has taught me. And this time, I know He got it right with Adam. I understand the value of our relationship because of the lessons of my past.

Everyone has a past. Learn from it.

Coming Together

My anxiety is slightly at ease.

Gently breathing in and out, I close my laptop and go straight to the kitchen. It is around six o'clock on a Friday evening and the sky is getting dark. I got out of work early today, so it was nice to take a few extra hours to focus on my stories. Adam is going to be at my apartment in about an hour or so—I just need to see him. I need to tell him what I've been writing—tell him that every word and sentiment was real at one point in my life, but that every day moving forward is all him. *Only him.*

Adam is the person I am most afraid to share my stories with. No matter who reads my words, his thoughts mean everything to me. Especially since I was so transparent with my previous relationships. *Maybe I should have just let him read my diaries instead?* Too late. I'm already invested.

At the edge of my kitchen counter sits Ina Garten's recipe book, *Cooking for Jeffrey*, creased and practically worn out. Whenever I need a break from words, I bake. So, I open the book for the thousandth time with my stale fingers and weary eyes and find a recipe that I know I have the ingredients to. Peach cobbler.

After writing for hours and escaping to my past, it's necessary to escape to something else for a while. Besides, I can follow a recipe pretty well, if I do say so myself.

An hour passes and I hear my door buzz. It must be Adam because he texted me fifteen minutes earlier to ask if I had a wine preference for the night. I told him kisses and peach cobbler pair perfectly with any wine.

I open the door. My apartment smells of bread and butter. Only a half hour until the cobbler is ready.

"That was a cute joke you texted me," he says. His smile is so beautiful.

He kisses me and I begin to peel away the goodies he has brought: a bottle of wine and a pizza box from Grimaldi's for us to devour. It is movie night for us so, I made sure to wear my coziest socks.

Sitting down with him at my counter, swapping plates to accommodate pizza slice sizes, I feel my heart pound a little harder at the idea of telling him about my book. About all the boys and stories before him. About who I used to be.

"Adam, I need to tell you something," I say. I look at my pizza slice as those words stumble out of my mouth.

He is mid-bite, with cheese oozing from his folded slice hold. Eyes wide while chewing down the cheese, he makes a quick smirk and laughs. I laugh too because he is just so cute.

"Is everything okay?" he says, looking weary and concerned.

"Everything is great! But I want to tell you about a project I have been working on."

His eyes are focused on me. Cell phones away, no distractions. This is my moment.

"You see," I gulp. "Ever since we found my journals, I've had this strange feeling that I needed to open them up again. It all started when you asked if you could read them. Do you remember that?"

He slowly nods his head. I can feel his eyes on my face. I can't bear to look at him at the moment. My anxiety is too much.

"Well, it gave me an idea for a book. A book called *Three*, signifying relationships in your life that help you figure out who you are. I know it sounds dumb, but I felt like I need to release my stories. Maybe it's me trying to break free? I feel like they can help people—even if just one person reads it."

My legs are shaking, and my heart is going a million miles a minute. I'm still not able to look at him.

"I also purchased my domain name, I am organizing my website, and I'm thinking about publishing my stories for the world to see. The problem is that I can't be this transparent with everyone without being transparent with you first."

I look at him. His eyes are on mine, and he smiles.

"I want you to read my stories before anyone else. Every part of each word has meaning. I share who I used to be and the stupidity of it all. I loved before you, you know that, but there has been no one I've ever loved more than you. It's important to me you know that."

Beep. Beep. The cobbler is ready. I immediately slip away to the opposite end of the counter and find my polka-dot oven mitts to pull out the peachy goodness. My heart is racing. I feel lightheaded at my confession. I feel like I really shouldn't be handling something hot at that moment.

I place the cobbler down on another part of the counter to cool off and feel two hands slip along my waist from behind me. I turn around to see Adam gently smile at me and kiss my forehead. As we embrace, a feeling of relief overcomes me. I shed a tear, look back at him, and smile.

Instead of movies, we spend the night reading my stories, talking, giggling, and enjoying each other's company. It opens up a conversation about his past and the memories that shaped him. We realize how each of our paths aligned and how our experiences led us to find each other. He is proud of me and my stories.

That night, he holds me close. We laugh over cobbler, kiss each other goodnight, and go to bed.

I remember the days when all I ever wanted in life was a Barbie airplane. Now all I wish is for my friends and family to be happy. Adam and I continue to be in a healthy relationship together, and to be right with God. All my prayers and dreams revolve around love in some shape or form. And now that Adam knows the truth about me, I feel okay writing all of this down for you to see.

As we grow, our hearts change, and our minds toughen up. We seek out the more important things in life and realize that what we perceived as problems when we were young weren't really problems, just stepping-stones. They were the pieces we needed to complete life's jigsaw puzzle.

I'm going to ask you to reflect on your life, just for a bit. In doing so, I hope the heartache has made you stronger and your experiences bring a smile to your face. I hope you get a laugh thinking about all of the crazy stuff you used to do when you were younger. I hope you have found forgiveness for your mistakes and recognize that everything happened for a reason and that life is just going to keep getting better with time. *I hope all of this for you.*

So now that I have spilled the words and thoughts from my journals, I want to leave you with these words to remember:

Learn to say yes to yourself and say no to others when necessary.

Read that again.

This isn't meant to be the typical self-help lesson of learning to love yourself first—even though that is true—but a matter of being selfish with your time when you are young and learning from your mistakes as you get older. Even as an adult, I still see family members searching for who they are and sometimes it's a struggle to watch. Just remember that there is always hope. Don't feel like your time has run out yet.

Regarding romantic relationships, sometimes you have to get your heart broken by someone else because it's better than having yourself break your own heart by not living the life you deserve. When it comes to your goals and aspirations, just go for it, and do your best—it's better to live your life trying than to live life with regret. Life comes at you from all angles, but there is no doubt that you can overcome any obstacle brought along your path.

Regarding what I said earlier about being selfish with your time. This does not mean to be insincere and not think of others along your journey.

Instead, learn to prioritize your faith and yourself with the time that you do have—especially when you are young and figuring things out. No journey is completed alone. You have a responsibility to yourself to do what is best for you, but don't forget to ask for help along the way. I think all of us are guilty of not asking for help and for thinking that we need to do it all on our own. That's simply not true. Make yourself proud and listen to your brain—not just your heart—and find your support with faith, friends, and family.

When you are in a relationship that is making you stray away from your beliefs and motivations, it's time to reevaluate your situation and pray about it. Some women and men stay stuck in their toxic situations because it's hard to let go or because it's convenient, but I'm telling you it's possible to break free.

Although I know that every person's journey is different, I do believe that every relationship, struggle, achievement, and heartache is always placed along your path for a reason. Whether to grow or learn, the people that you surround yourself with in life and the decisions that you make truly affect your being in a mighty way. But you know what else is even more powerful? Prayer. Prayer is powerful—especially when you're growing and learning.

I am not a perfect Catholic, obviously. I haven't memorized the Bible, I have told a few lies in my life, and as you have already read, I've done many things that I would be terrified of my future daughter doing. However, I am proud of who I am becoming and the lessons I can pass on to my siblings, future children, and other people that I meet along life's journey. I couldn't teach them these lessons without experiencing, learning, and owning up to my mistakes. So now as I wrap this up, I want to remind you that it's okay to feel lost— but you will be found. Your faith will lead you along your intended path and I promise you it will be worth it.

Just like my mom says, it's not how you start, but how you finish.

Don't worry about anything, but instead, pray about everything.
— Philippians 4:6

Acknowledgments

Nothing in life would be possible without your love, support, and precious guidance. Every one of you has given me a life full of joy and countless blessings. You are what motivates me every single day.

Rudy and Claudia Peña
Jose and Teresa Guerra
Juan Guerra
Monica Guerra Lopez
Luis Guerra

Martha Guerra
Mathew Peña
Christopher Peña
Lexie Peña

Michael,
Your love epitomizes every fairytale and dream. You are my greatest
blessing. I love you, forever.

CPSIA information can be obtained
at www.ICGtesting.com
Printed in the USA
LVHW091355030921
696883LV00020B/994/J